Advance Praise for *The Middle Fork*

"Blending outdoor adventure and hot-button politics is Rick Glaze's game in *The Middle Fork*. This is a timely exploration of today's issues wrapped in a suspenseful story."

—Paul Nyberg, publisher, *Los Altos Town Crier*

"A taut adventure in which politics and a river merge in unusual ways."

—Fred Lowell, former chairman, Northern California Lincoln Club

"The Middle Fork is an artful combination of spine-chilling adventure and red-hot politics...a must read."

—Duf Sundheim, former Chairman, California Republican Party

"The Middle Fork is a white water, white knuckle adventure with a splash of romance and politics masterfully blended."

—Luis Buhler, Bay Area Vice Chairman, California Republican Party

"Flash floods, romance, and a battle royal of politics—*The Middle Fork* has it all. I couldn't put it down."

—Jerry Ceppos, Dean, Reynolds School of Journalism, University of Nevada, Reno
Former executive editor, *San Jose Mercury News*
Former vice president for news, Knight Ridder Corporation

"An interesting cross-genre book. I haven't read anything like it before, and I enjoyed it thoroughly. It makes you think, while completely entertaining you."

—Tom Campbell, former dean, Haas School of Business, University of California, Berkeley; former U.S. congressman

Dick Glaze
August 24, 2009

The Middle Fork

A POLITICAL NOVEL

Rick Glaze

Synergy Books

The Middle Fork
Published by Synergy Books
P.O. Box 80107
Austin, Texas 78758

For more information about our books, please write to us, call 512.478.2028, or visit our website at www.synergybooks.net.

Publisher's Cataloging-in-Publication
(Provided by Quality Books, Inc.)
Glaze, Rick.
   The middle fork : a political novel / Rick Glaze.
   p. cm.
   LCCN 2008909214
   ISBN-13: 978-0-9821601-0-7
   ISBN-10: 0-9821601-0-0

   1. Kayaking--Idaho--Salmon River--Fiction. 2. Salmon
River (Idaho)--Fiction. 3. Adventure stories, American.
4. Political fiction, American. 5. Psychological
fiction, American. I. Title.

PS3607.L385M53 2009   813'.6
                  QBI08-600302

This is a work of fiction. All of the characters and events portrayed in this book are fictional, and any resemblance to real people or incidents is purely coincidental.

Cover concept design by Dan Yeager.

10 9 8 7 6 5 4 3 2 1

Preface

There is an old saying, "wherever you go, there you are." I've been lucky enough to enjoy the thrill and excitement of running rapids on some of America's greatest rivers. And on every rafting trip I've run, people have brought their lives, thoughts, and biases with them. As those who have taken these trips know, the physical and psychological thrills and dangers of a white-water adventure swiftly replace the cares of everyday life. As the pace of life shifts, the conversations also change, often to issues that are of great importance to those on the trip. I have experienced, firsthand, many of the conversations that happen in *The Middle Fork*, and I was struck by the passion and intensity we as individuals hold about the future of our country and our world. There is nothing like taking a brief postponement from your hot debate on the Iraq war so you can run Blossom Gorge Rapids. And through this unique venue of dialogue, some of the lucky ones are able to abandon a few pieces of old baggage in the crevices and crannies along the riverbank.

Politics can seem like a black-and-white proposition, one side or the other, my side or his side, red state or blue state. But the answers to all the contentious controversies of our time lie somewhere in the middle, and we as people need to be willing to step out of our respective wings to find the solutions. The United States is unique in its promise to foster political discussion and welcome discourse as a tool for progress. I believe Americans need to find a dialogue, a place to incubate common-ground solutions. Our culture, history, and spirit require that we establish a model for our citizens and the rest of the world, not just to win debates, but to solve problems—and there are plenty to solve.

Through the characters in this book, I tried to highlight issues that I am particularly passionate about, and endeavored to be an advocate for those issues that I believe are critical to our future prosperity. Readers may be fully aware of the intricacies of topics like global warming or immigration, or they may have only heard of an issue and know little detail. Either way, these real-life emotional contests between personalities will rivet you and draw into question your stand on these important concerns. And, maybe a few lucky ones will leave a little old baggage tucked away behind a rock where nobody can find it. *The Middle Fork* awaits you with plenty of adventure and plenty of food for thought.

Acknowledgments

The first thanks goes to the great team at Synergy Books for their editing and handholding and for sharing my vision for this book, and to Phenix and Phenix Literary Publicists for getting the word out. Thanks to Stanford University's Creative Writing Program and especially to Stephanie Reents, who told me "you can't write your second one, until you write your first one." So in a way, this is really all her fault. Thanks to Stephanie too for editing drafts one, two, and three and softening up my punchy style.

Special thanks to the river runners who ran the rapids with me all these years. Great thanks to Barry Elkins for organizing most of the trips, including the Salmon River trip. Thanks to Orange Torpedo River Adventures for welcoming us every year and to Arizona Raft Adventures for two great runs down the Grand Canyon. Thanks to Amanda Glaze for taking a chance on kayaking and joining me for the Salmon trip and for never taking anything I say at face value, but requiring proof for everything. Thanks to Georgia Glaze for making each trip a delight, and special acknowledgement to my wife, Nancy, for not rolling her eyes when I announced I was going to write a novel and for reading all the drafts. Thanks to Steve Rankin for lessons on the Zen of fishing.

Thanks to all the members of the Northern California Lincoln Club and SPARC for bringing in great speakers and cutting-edge political seminars that helped my characters fine-tune their debates.

1

I waited with Sonia in the flat water above while the first group cleared the rapid. Derek, our guide, paddled vigorously as he hit and pierced the first small wave. A slight back paddle jerked the front of his boat to the left so he would hit the next wave at a right angle. The bow of the air-filled craft punched through the short standing wave, and with a swift stroke on each side, he accelerated through into the quiet water. Simon spun out just above the rapid, and while he recovered, the fast current carried Mike past him into the first wave. The curl hit his bow on the left side, peppered his face with spray, and started to roll the boat back to the right. Mike leaned into the wave, thrust his paddle into the dinky water wall, and jerked it toward him, leveling his boat as he burst through to the flat water. His paddle blade cut through the water's surface on the right side, and he accelerated toward the next target. Like Derek, he back paddled on the left, hitting the next wave at a perpendicular angle. Ripping through the wave, he raised his paddle, opened his mouth, and gave a "rebel yell" that echoed through the river canyon.

Regaining control above the rapid, Simon turned his boat downstream to hit the first swell, dead-on straight. The puny wave was no match for his 240 pounds, and it flattened like an insignificant ripple under his weight. Looking pleased and confident, he steered his boat into the second wave, and the small water wall hit his left side. His broad shoulders and torso, which carried most of his weight, unsettled the boat's balance, and the top-heavy craft lurched to the right. Simon leaned with the boat's momentum, away from the wave, helping the boat roll over and gently lay him in the soft, wet trough that made up the hole.

The current swept Keith's boat into the rapids behind Simon. As he punched through the first wave, the soft rubber bow of his boat was thrust by the current into Simon's boat and over the top of his chest, lodging snuggly into the center of the capsizing craft. The calm water of the trough kept Keith in his boat for a second or two as both boats moved into the pounding curl of the small wave. Like Simon, Keith was laid into the water as if a mother were placing her baby in a warm bath. But even the small wave had enough momentum under the surface to shove both men to the frigid river bottom. They cleared the swirling undertow and popped up like corks clad in crimson life jackets about six feet downstream.

Derek grabbed the shoulder panels of Simon's jacket as he surfaced into the swirling, churning currents and tugged the deadweight of Simon's drenched body over the front of his own boat with ease. Another river guide floated alongside with Simon's boat tethered to his line, helping Simon as he struggled to pull himself into his rescued craft and settle into the small seat.

"What the hell were you doing up there?" Keith shouted. "You almost killed me." He was back in his boat, the current propelling him toward Simon and Derek. He turned his head as he passed to maintain eye contact with Simon. "This is supposed to be a vacation, not a funeral. Look, if you can't cut it, stay out of my way."

Simon was still gasping for air, savoring each precious breath. "Should I give him the finger or just paddle over and bash the little twerp's head in? It might put him out of his misery and do the world a big favor." Tumbling into the cold, choppy water had separated him from his up and down orientation as well as from his top and bottom. He was unnerved, but Simon, who usually paused before he spoke, was not the kind of man to be browbeaten. He was mostly bald, but a well-oiled comb-over covered the center of his head. The bones of his cranium formed small canyons and plateaus, and the back part of his head flattened in a diagonal plain to the ground. His coloring was dark, and his face was clean shaven.

"Let it go," called a voice from just upriver. "He wears his emotions on his sleeve. He's just a little jumpy, that's all." Mike floated into view from behind Simon.

"Emphasis on 'emotion,' I guess."

"Keith is a client of mine. He's okay," Mike said with cordial resolve.

"I can let it go, Mike, but that guy needs to mellow out or it will be a long week."

"He will," Mike replied. "Everybody mellows out on the river after a few days.

"I hope you're right." Simon paused and began to paddle slowly. "But anyway, these dinky little blowup kayaks aren't exactly my ticket. I mean, they feel top heavy and unstable."

"Well, they're not the best for pros, but they're probably the best for our level."

"Best for what? They're flimsy and cheap."

"But you don't have to know how to roll in the rapids," I said, "because you can't get stuck, just thrown out."

"Yeah, I noticed," Simon said. "You know, when Mike said river trip, I thought he meant this would be like my trip down the Grand Canyon. I mean, seven paddlers in a raft digging into those massive curls. I've seen the front guys take the brunt of two giant waves in close succession and get leveled onto the floor of the raft and lucky not to be thrown out and swimming. But everyone else is there to keep digging, so you take whatever the river can throw at you and learn to beat the old matron at her own game."

I looked over to the side and saw a quiet, steady river streaming past a steep, muddy bank. Mostly young saplings gazed out on the constant motion of the river's rush to the sea. The roots of one ancient oak punched through the dirty bank, penetrating the humid air and curving like a giant elbow back down into the rushing water. It looked like a wise old gentleman among a free-for-all of youth. But, of course, it wasn't. It was just an old tree surviving in a rugged wilderness.

Why Simon was calling the river a "her" was beyond me. Was it for the same reason hurricanes were named after females for years? Maybe it was once thought of as a compliment? Or maybe it was a character trait reflected in the big storm, as in "there is no wrath like a woman's scorn" type of allusion. But I remembered that old song about the Mississippi River, "Old Man River." Where is the wrath on the Mississippi River? I guess the Mississippi is a big slow river that "just keeps rollin' along," but the Grand Canyon has the wrath of a woman, and likewise there would be some trouble on this stretch of the smaller Salmon River. Wrath we could take, I mused; mayhem is harder.

I paddled downriver and caught up with Sonia. She was a striking sandy blonde who looked athletic but possessed a girlish charm. As my boat pulled up from behind, I saw the even, steady stroke of her paddling, a straight back, and a poised demeanor. It looked like she practiced yoga. She was the kind of woman I wish I had met in my youth. But then I stopped; I knew better than to fool myself. Back then, I was looking for meaning, depth, and sensitivity. I dated girls who were artists and poets and, as it turns out, were mostly tortured by their emotions and those of various populations around the world that they never even met, just like a poet is supposed to be. Karen, the girl I married, was an artist, completely the opposite of Sonia. She was a good companion and did a good job with the kids, but her idea of recreation was having tea and chatting. She had a close circle of friends and was reluctant to expand her group. I liked a little broader reach and had friends but also a lot of acquaintances, people I would hang out with but didn't really know. All the same, I was happy with the few friends Karen had and the "good" friendships she kept up. But I was a different person back then, before Karen died.

Sonia seemed youthful and energetic, but I wondered what she was really like.

"Hi there," I said, trying to be low-key and easygoing. "Well, we're off. It should be exciting."

"You're Jonathan, right?"

I nodded.

"Yeah, it'll be fun if the boys don't kill each other," Sonia replied.

"So you heard the little altercation?"

"Not the whole thing, but I got the general picture. What is the old saying, 'wherever you go, there you are'?"

"Yeah, give it a little time," I said. "They'll start playing nice. They've all been out on rivers before."

Sonia looked ahead and quietly paddled her kayak, floating down with the slow-moving current. Her eyes stayed down-river until she turned her head and in a gentle, quiet voice, like the rhythm of the river, answered, "I have never been on a river trip where I thought everybody there should be there, or that everybody understood the level of extreme sport this is. It's like a hurricane—the river can be unforgiving and indiscriminant, and good times can go bad quick."

And like a woman, I thought, you want to enjoy its beauty but give it constant respect. I had heard of catastrophes and helicopter evacuations on these trips but had never seen one. We all expected some big waves and some very big "holes" that could suck you down before spitting you back out to the surface. Some people expected it more than others. But everybody would be fine, I thought.

2

hundred miles east in the Bitterroot Mountain Range separating Idaho from Montana, a thundercloud blocked out the sun and turned a cool summer morning into nearly night. Summer storms are common in the mountains, where the rainfall can reach sixty inches a year, but this weather front covered one hundred fifty miles north to south and promised a real soaking. The mountain range between the little towns of Salmon, Idaho, and Butte, Montana, are rugged, desolate, and claim only two or three people per square mile. The weather in this remote area is of little interest around the state, and the news reports barely mentioned the storm.

The runoff started in the high mountain canyons as flows so small you could hardly call them streams, but each trickle of water joined a nearby colleague to form narrow torrents that cut through the hilly crevices, giving in to gravity's pull to lower ground. Allan Mountain and Pyramid Peak are both more than nine thousand feet high, and the rain slipped off the mountain surfaces like butter off a hot knife. To the east on the Montana side, the South Fork of the Bitterroot River flowed north meeting up with the Flathead River, all dumping into Flathead Lake. The flow to the west found the Salmon River, which drains fourteen thousand square miles of wilderness. The Middle Fork joins the Main after a hundred and six miles through one of the deepest gorges in North America. One inch of rain in the mountains can cause these rivers to rise two feet downstream. The rain started about eight thirty in the morning and pelted the mountains with two inches of liquid sunshine in the first hour.

3

The sandy knoll grew from the water's edge at a lazy bend in the river. Thirty feet inland was a stand of scruffy trees that shaded the fine, cream-colored sand from the burning July sun. I alternated paddle strokes on the right and then left, pausing after each pull of the blade, mostly letting the current take me down the wide, calm stretch. I counted five class two and one class three rapids for our first day. The class threes have the big holes, which are two- or three-foot crevices that form directly in front of a standing wave. The waves curl back into the river in an upstream direction, forming a wall of water that can rise three or four feet. The lightweight kayaks we rode sunk into the hole and, if navigated correctly, and with enough force, punched through the curl to the water beyond. On this first day, Keith made it through the top of the first class three but was off balance and tippy, and turning sideways, he fell out and rode the rest of it in a cold shiver next to his boat. Simon ran two of the class twos well but swam the rest involuntarily, and when his boat beached on the sandbar, he looked spent and exhausted. The cold water and fear of another swim down the rapids was evident in his almost lifeless frame sprawled on the beach. The guides, led by Derek, explained the general strategy before each run but were clearly resolved that it was easier to dredge the fallen boaters out of the rapids and back into their boats than to make everybody an expert river rat in one day. I had followed Mike down most of the big ones and copied as much of what he did as I could, so I made it through the afternoon dry and in pretty good shape. As my boat approached the shore, I saw Mike standing on the sandy beach, winding up for an underhanded pitch.

"Take a load off with this, big guy." From Mike's hand a sparkling projectile accelerated toward me with precision aim befitting a great athlete. My hands let the paddle drop to the gunnels of my boat, and I instinctively reached over my head with my right hand and plucked the silver bullet from its parabolic flight path. As I brought it down, my left hand found the pull top and I yanked open the first beer of the day, a much-deserved reward. Mike gave a mild yell. Keith shrugged. Sonia ignored it, and Simon, after briefly standing, again collapsed on the sand.

4

Mike was my roommate in college and one of the most outgoing guys in the fraternity. While he was not the face man in the house, he could charm the chrome off a trailer hitch. He was an economics major but filled his electives with philosophy courses that he would rarely talk about except after a lot of beer, and then he couldn't get much conversation going because nobody else in the fraternity ever went near a philosophy course. Over the last twenty years, he built a huge business as a stockbroker in Hollywood, but he liked to stay light about life. Every few months I'd get a call from Mike.

"Hey, big guy, how is the young, nubile talent count in your office these days?" he would ask.

We hung on to the lingo of our fraternity days not because we lived it anymore or because Mike or I took any interest in the "eye candy" but because we got to escape for a few seconds to a time we could never replace and weren't all that happy to let go.

"Have you been river rafting since your Grand Canyon trip a few years ago?" he asked.

"Been thinking about it, but I never have carved out the time," I replied. "Do I sense a proposition coming on?"

"I've got a client who is a nut for river trips. Anyway, he went down the middle fork of the Salmon River last summer and is completely worked up about going down the main fork this year. He's putting together a small private trip with a guide service from the local area, but this time it's in one-man kayaks. Interested?"

"Is that in Montana?" I asked.

"Close, buddy-boy. It's in Idaho."

"Where's Idaho, anyway?" I quipped.

"It's about four hours by plane and about two weeks by mule train, smartass," he retorted.

I loved it when Mike called. We had a storehouse of inside jokes that never got old.

"Seen Muffin lately?" he would ask.

"No, but I can smell the aroma of that lovely flower around every corner."

And we would both break out in garish hilarity—over what? Over nothing, just the thought of Muffin, who was a party queen hanging around the frat house for our last two years. She was a girl back then, but now she was a symbol of the way we were but would never be again. It would be just a phone call, and it was always over too soon.

Mike's friend, Keith, took care of all the logistics and organized the trip. He was a biology professor at the University of California in Riverside. Mike's clients all have small fortunes, and Keith wouldn't be in that category on a professor's salary. But around ten years ago, he wrote a book about global warming that took off like a shot. It was perfect timing because the issue started getting front-page coverage in the major media just about that time. He made millions and became a poster boy for the cause. The guy was on TV for a year, it seemed, and on the lecture circuit, he was the star du jour. That book was considered pivotal because it outlined the primary concepts of the movement of global warming. Back then it was a theory loosely put together by a few, at the time they seemed radical, scientists, but Keith's book pulled it all together, and then slowly the theory seemed to become a fact. The whole idea of sunlight trapped by a layer of pollution seemed reasonable to me. Temperature variations on the planet and the history of these cycles is a field I know absolutely nothing about, but the global warming thing seemed to have substance to it. There's the pollution that comes along with progress, but when it starts affecting the atmosphere and the polar caps, it needs to be addressed. Keith was low-key about his success, but his general nature was high-strung and prone to argument. Mike made sure everybody knew how to get along with him. All the guys had been briefed, and everybody seemed cool about it.

Simon had some history with Mike running rivers, and he was an affable guy with a big heart. Born in Iran, he moved to Seattle at the age of ten when his father landed a job in the aerospace industry at Boeing. The U.S.-friendly Shah of Iran was overthrown just after that, and the radical religious sects took control of the country. According to Mike, Simon went back to Iran a few times as an adult, but they must have been secret trips because he never talked about the details.

An oncologist specializing in ovarian cancer in Los Angeles, Simon was in private practice with five doctors. His affiliation with the UCLA Medical Center was his introduction to Mike as a financial advisor. Simon was jovial and easygoing with a hyena cackle of a laugh that some people thought was infectious, but I always thought sounded a little forced or fabricated. He was a good guy, don't get me wrong, but like everybody, I figured Simon had some layers of the onion skin that concealed deep secrets.

The big wildcard for the trip was Sonia. She was a friend of Simon's daughter, Alicia, and the two of them were signed on for the trip. But Alicia had a bad tennis accident two days before the trip and had to cancel. The assumption was that Sonia wouldn't want to spend a week floating down the river with a bunch of middle-aged guys who were old enough to be her father, but when the group arrived at the airport in Los Angeles, there she was quietly waiting and ready to go. Simon knew her because she had hung out with Alicia a few times at his backyard swimming pool. He had been extremely reluctant to go himself because Alicia's injuries were severe. She was a tennis pro at the Bel-Air Country Club. During a warm-up game, she charged the net to return a volley. Her feet tangled and she crashed onto the court, shattering her elbow and fracturing her knee. Simon's wife, who never went on outdoor adventures with him, convinced everybody she had everything under control, and even Alicia insisted that Simon and Sonia both go.

Sonia was thirty-four, with an MBA from the Anderson School of Business at UCLA, and a political journalist for the *American Patriot*, a conservative weekly periodical. She was single and appeared to be very happy with that—comfortable in her own skin, so to speak. Her five-foot, four-inch frame supported a sandy blond head of hair, cut in an attractive, outdoorsy style, a thin straight nose that looked a little Scandinavian, and fair skin dotted with a few small freckles on the edge of her high cheeks.

The first time I saw her, she was standing in the back of a crowded bar in Salmon, Idaho. I had just arrived by cab from the small airport, fresh in on a puddle jumper from Boise, and I had no idea she was going down the river with us. The L.A. group had been there a couple of hours when I strolled into the watering hole. A light mounted on the wall illuminated the right side of her face, and her profile was striking, almost taking my breath away. After greeting Mike and the others, I tried to work my way over to her, figuring I'd never see her again, but Keith buttonholed me to talk about real estate investing as she slipped out the front door and disappeared.

5

erek meandered into the light of the campfire. He was looking around, probably for Sonia, I thought. There was no doubt he had noticed her. They were about the same age, and let's face it, the young ones are on the lookout for each other. I glanced up from my hamburger and baked beans to see him bring a small guitar up under his right arm and strum a chord.

"'Kumbaya,' anyone?" he said with a sheepish grin.

He was svelte and muscular at about five feet, five inches tall. His short, brown hair had an unkempt wilderness look with fashionable sideburns extending below his ears. Nine summers guiding river trips had turned his skin a dark bronze tone, which glowed in the light of the dancing flames. Derek entertained for half an hour with campfire songs. When he strummed, "I'm An Old Cow Hand from the Rio Grande," one of the guides pulled a box of strike-matches out of his pocket and began to shake them along with the song's beat. My foot patted out the rhythm as I settled into a welcomed slow groove.

The large birch log I sat on must have washed up during some high-water rainy season in the last decade or so. Smooth knobs were all that remained of once-majestic branches long ago broken off and honed by a relentless river flow. The rippled exterior was split by long cracks running its length and traversing the white, sun-bleached surface. Dead lichen clung to the shattered ends like old glue. Mine was not the only polished log anchored to the shore. The small ones got thrown on the fire, but the big ones rooted out a lifeless foundation in the sand, finding a place to rest and to watch the world unfold.

The campfire smoldered with a red glow, and when the song ended, Keith said in a low voice, "It's good to be in the wilderness and out of California."

"Yeah, the quiet out here is deafening," I said more to the fire than to Keith. Tomorrow is the third day out of the city, I thought, and the three-day rule always works. Three days to unwind. I could feel the dull buzz of civilization in my ears fading away. The subtle sounds of the river at night were becoming more vivid. Wilderness was the right place to be. I was almost me again. Nobody's calling me "sir," no meetings to run or bankers to cajole. Just paddle myself down the river on my own and everybody else would take care of themselves. I was so overwhelmed with delight that I leaned as far as I could to my right, reached into the ice chest, and pulled out another beer. Here's to day three, I thought.

Keith pierced my tranquility. "It's really good to get away from all the controversies. California—and the whole country, for that matter—is a mess." He paused. "It's not just the environment that bothers me. There are a lot of issues that get me riled. For one, this immigration issue is ugly, and the state's radical right wing has destroyed affirmative action and set minorities back fifty years. Jesus, I just need a break from it all. I guess everybody needs a break, right?"

I could tell the buzz in Keith's ears was more like a vise around his head. He might need three weeks to unwind.

"What did you think of our first day on the river, Keith?" I said, trying to change the subject back to a more pleasant topic. The water was gently slapping the sandbar, and the night air was cooling rapidly, but Keith was giving me a different kind of chill.

Ignoring my question, he said, "I mean, the state's being overrun by fanatics."

I took a deep breath, and though my mind felt silent, my mouth started to move: "I'm not an expert on the subject, but I thought eliminating affirmative action in the state universities, if that's what you are talking about, was passed by a state initiative that everybody in California voted on."

"Well, the initiative was put on the ballot by right-wing radicals. And now you have to be a citizen to get public services. I mean they're 'public,' right? Come on, this is about people not about numbers," he countered.

"That initiative passed by sixty percent or so, and California is over-the-top liberal. Where do you get this right-wing radical thing?"

"America was based on opening its arms to the poor and downtrodden, those less fortunate, those that need us. Look at the Irish, the Italians, and the Japanese. They immigrated and have assimilated. We have to be inclusive," Keith continued.

"Didn't those groups assimilate into American culture and society over a generation or two?" I posed.

"That's what I'm talking about—inclusive, open arms. Everything we as a country and a society stand for," he said.

I wondered if I should make one more attempt to change the subject or just find my tent and crash. Keith was a thinking, caring person who wanted to do the right thing, but his type argue with their hearts on their sleeves. I had a policy not to tangle with them, because there is never a winner. As soon as you trot out a few facts that prove them wrong, they change the subject or try to pull out juicy details that are over your head. No winning there.

A voice from behind me pierced the brief silence. "But there isn't an open border between California and Italy, Keith. Italian children learned to speak English and live the American way of life and have become Americans. The Mexican border is wide open. Vast numbers of people go back and forth freely, never assimilating, never learning the language, and never becoming productive citizens."

Keith looked over his left shoulder and saw Sonia standing in the faint light of the low smoldering fire.

"Where did you come from?" he said slightly under his breath with an irritated grimace on his face. His chin dropped as his head turned toward the fire.

I looked up, away from the fire, and could see the dense cloud cover that blanketed most of the night sky. Low in the west, the clouds broke slightly, and the three stars that formed the top of Orion's belt peeked through. My mind fixed for half a second on a sense of wholeness and forever, the beginning and the end, not just the details in the middle, ideas that a determined, successful businessman running his own company has little time for.

"Well I'm not a spokes-*man*, Keith," Sonia fired back. "I'm a woman, and I've been sitting on this log watching the fire since before you guys started your little political contest, and I hate it when grown men distort simple facts and then argue they're true." She tried to smile to soften her delivery, but it had little effect.

"Listen, Sonia, people need a chance. There are no opportunities for people in Mexico. That's why they come here. We're the land of opportunity. That's what we cherish and fight to protect," Keith said.

"The upper classes in Mexico, who try their damndest to keep the Spanish bloodlines pure, pay no attention to the peasants looking for 'opportunity.' In fact, they're happy to have the good old U.S. of A. take care of them. Mexico is a textbook case of racism, Keith, Jesus Christ! The Mexican government is even encouraging duel citizenship. They can vote twice," Sonia said. "Then you have a whole group of whining lunatics who want the schools to teach in their native language, so they have no chance of assimilating and no chance of finding prosperity in our country. The Italians and the Chinese kids weren't taught in their native language, and the result is that those groups became part of America and its opportunities," she continued.

"Wait a minute, groups of lunatics is a bit—"

Sonia cut him off. "You ideologues want a nice, fresh group of dependent, downtrodden people you can subjugate, who will feel obligated to vote for your pious candidates. If immigrants succeed in the American dream, they might learn the benefits of self-reliance, hard work, and personal responsibility and not vote for your candidates."

Derek appeared in front of the fire, pulled his guitar up under his arm, and strummed a few chords. He wasn't exactly interrupting the conversation, but trying to avert a potential train wreck.

Faint lightening flashes illuminated the dense cloud cover in the eastern sky. The low ceiling appeared out of the darkness like a blanket overhead. It looked like a storm was going to unleash on the eastern mountain range. Maybe it wouldn't come over this far, but we could handle some rain on the river if it did. It just meant the sun wouldn't be drying us off and warming us up. But in any case, it was better than being in the office back home.

Everybody was silent for a brief moment, and I could hear the river flowing. The steady sound of the water settled my mind. During the winter when it rained more often, I guessed that the sound was different, maybe a higher-pitched roar, but it was still steady and the river didn't seem to care about politics or offices or colleges or even Muffin. The steady droning sound of the water bouncing off the rocks and the riverbanks probably sounded the same when Caesar crossed the Rubicon in 6 BC, when Washington crossed the Delaware in 1776, and the same when…when Jose crossed the Rio Grande last night. I wished they would talk about something else.

Keith broke the calm. "The Democratic Party has plenty of solid backers, and they don't need to manufacture support from the 'downtrodden,' as you put it. Some of the greatest institutions of our country are the result of the progressive thinking of the Democratic Party. Corporations were polluting the drinking water, the air, and the ocean at a devastating pace before the environmental movement started. And we need this movement. If fossil fuel emission continues at this rate, the planet will heat the ice caps and flood the major continents in ten years. Kiss civilization good-bye."

Derek interjected. "I don't want to interrupt your guys' fun, but I've read some scary stuff about the polar ice caps affected by pollution from smokestacks and cars."

"Carbon emissions are increasing as more countries industrialize," Keith added.

"Mostly from cars, right? Electricity is clean?" Derek asked.

"Cars are a big part of it, but power plants producing electricity put a lot of carbon in the atmosphere," Keith responded.

"But most new electric plants in the U.S. these days are natural-gas fired," Sonia chimed in, "so they burn cleaner."

"Okay, Sonia, listen carefully. I'm going to give you a little lesson in economics straight from the world of hard knocks," Keith said slowly with a hint of sarcasm. "Power plants are mostly built to use the fuel source that is most available and most economical in that particular region. Transportation is very advanced in the developed countries, so pipelines carry oil and gas around the U.S. and Canada. But in China, for example, where the economic growth is so rapid and transportation is less developed, plants are being rushed into service in areas where coal is the only plentiful energy source. Factories are producing everything from can openers to iPods, and the population is demanding a higher lifestyle. This translates into more gadgets that run on electricity. Smokestacks are billowing carbon into the atmosphere in order to keep up with electricity demand."

"But the scientific reality is that it's hard to relate that directly to climate change," Sonia said.

Simon jumped into the conversation. "The climate has been changing for centuries, long before smokestacks."

"So what! I can't see why filling the atmosphere with this much pollution is an acceptable thing anyway," Mike said.

"The coastal cities in the world could be flooded in ten years from polar melting plus growth in the oceans' volume just from heat expansion," Keith said.

"Climate change can't go that quick," Sonia said. "It's a longer-term cycle."

"This one could," Keith replied.

The air felt moist as the rain threatened, but the damp blanket on the conversation was Keith's dire prediction. He, by far, was the expert in this field, and no one wanted to take it any further, even Sonia. It was quiet for a while, and I could feel Keith basking in the glory of his triumph. *El profesor* had spoken. I thought the heavy topics were over for the night, and hopefully for the rest of the trip, but Keith was on a roll and wanted to take advantage of his position to make a few essential points for our nightcap. Though a little friendly argument was fine even in the wilderness, this contest seemed out of place and even vicious, but Keith and Sonia were both relishing in the fight. They were like champion boxers with years of training and skill, sparing, eager to see what the competition could throw back, to see how to deflect a jab and counter with a knockout punch.

"There are other social struggles that are taken for granted today," Keith proceeded. "Like racial integration that the Democratic Party fought for in the sixties and seventies, pitted against the right-wing zealots in the Southern states."

Sonia glanced at Derek, and with a slight tilt of her head, seemed to acknowledge his effort to get things on a neutral track. He gave a halfhearted sheepish grin and turned his eyes toward the fire. Here it is, I thought, the multiple-front attack strategy. Keith's strongest argument was bound to be the global warming area, but he was lobbing a few grenades over the whole playing field, just for fun.

"Before you get carried away," Sonia said, "let me point out that the Southern states were dominated by the Democratic Party at that time and had been since the Civil War ended. Republicans were despised as 'carpetbaggers,' people who came down from the North to enforce integration. It was an ugly period, and integration didn't work all that well. But the feelings stuck for a hundred years, and when a young James Meredith tried to enroll in the all-white University of Mississippi, it was the Democrat governor, Ross Barnett, who blocked the way."

Sonia was beginning to preach, I thought. But her command of these topics was impressive, and she wasn't going to let broad swipes go unchallenged. I found her tenacity and determination attractive in a way, and kind of a turn-on. But I kept telling myself to leave it alone; she was too young.

I did want them to end this tit for tat, but I sat there like a statue transfixed by the conversation, not remembering who was governor of Mississippi in 1965. Hell, I'd never been to Mississippi. But the drama of this punching fest—and that's what it was—was hypnotizing like a bad B movie.

"Those were the wrong kind of Democrats," Keith said with a sarcastic smirk.

"Like Clarence Thomas, Colin Powell, and Condelezza Rice are the wrong kind of Blacks?" Sonia quipped.

Even in the low firelight, I could see Keith's face turning red. They were gearing up for some fireworks, and Keith was going to be the first one to blow, I thought.

Sonia continued, "Hey, Keith, there have been great accomplishments—like integration, environmental awareness, and my personal favorite, equality for women—opening up opportunities in education, sports, careers, and so on. But people who were progressive in those areas have passed their name tags on to champions of the status quo. Each year we graduate more kids than the year before from high school who can't read or write at a functional level. And who blocks education reform? The progressives. And who is a major constituency of the progressives? The teachers unions who don't want to have to redesign their curriculum just to pass a cold, faceless achievement test. They would rather produce generation after generation of welfare recipients."

"You're getting pretty hard core, Sonia," I interjected.

"The facts are what they are. I don't make them up," she answered. "The problem with the progressives is that they are not progressive anymore. New problems come up and new ways of thinking need to be nurtured. The liberals, who call themselves progressive, are just protecting their turf, no innovation, no new thinking."

Keith looked annoyed, to say it kindly. Actually, he looked like he might explode. Emotion was welling up in his face as Sonia's razor-sharp tongue was cutting deep. Something told me she and Muffin wouldn't have been friends.

"Hey, back to the environmental issues, I think Keith has a few good points," I said. "When we were growing up, big companies didn't take any responsibility for their waste or pollution. I, for one, am glad we have a new group running these companies and we have cleaner air and water."

I thought Sonia was making some good points, but Keith needed a little help just then.

"Well, they didn't do it on their own. I can promise you that," Keith said. "Hard-won battles by a dedicated group both in and out of the government brought about laws that protect everybody. Hell, the government was dumping nuclear waste in the Pacific Ocean. What were they thinking? Morons!" Keith continued in a strained, high-pitched voice. "At a gold mine in Montana, one of the containment units for hazardous byproducts broke apart, spilling mercury and arsenic that saturated the water table for miles. Children got deformities and cancer."

"It takes a different mindset to do manufacturing, and all business for that matter, in a clean, responsible way. But once that mindset is established, it becomes more a question of how to do business cleanly, not whether you do it cleanly," I said.

"It's naïve to think that big business will follow through on its own. They have to be made to conform. Corporate titans have one thing on their minds, and that is profit, and that always comes at the expense of the average citizen. Everybody knows that," Keith said.

He stood up when he said "corporate titan" and slowly paced in front of the fire. Having regained his ground, his delivery was professorial and confident, and his voice notched down to a lower register as he bent down and picked up a small log. He held it in front of him just below his line of vision. As he finished talking, his eyes dropped slightly, and he studied the log's craggy surface before tossing it into the center of the fire pit. The sun-dried log nuzzled a berth for itself in the red-hot bed of burning coals but did not immediately start to blaze. Meandering funnels of gray smoke cut a channel up into the dancing flames, escaping to the night sky.

Keith had opened up an ideological wound between liberals and conservatives that in my mind was long past being relevant in today's political dialogue. That is, "profit is evil." But just the same, it was a part of the heritage of the debate between the parties and was often used when no other good controversies were available. Some business man is always going to be caught doing the wrong thing to some group or another, but that doesn't make business a bad thing. God knows there is no shortage of politicians, or other public figures, running amuck or stealing the "little people's" money. Didn't I read that some United Way guy squandered millions, or did he just take it? I couldn't remember. If your philosophy of life was based on the rotten exceptions, everybody'd be in trouble. Eighty percent of working people in the country are employed by small businesses, and every one of those owners has to make a profit or employees are on the street. Communist Russia applied the "profit is bad" idea, and they utterly collapsed.

Sonia rose from her perch on a large, rounded bolder but changed her mind and sat back down. She shifted her right hip forward on the rock and seemed to find a more comfortable position. But I knew she was not going to find any comfort in the place Keith was going with this discussion. Derek jumped up, gave a cordial but understated nod to the group, and disappeared into the darkness. For an instant, I thought there would be no rebuttal from Sonia and the peace and tranquility of our rustic environs would prevail, but my hopes were dashed.

"Well, you dragged that one right out of ancient history. Profit is the backbone of a free-market economy. Capitalism is about investing in enterprises that make money," Sonia said in a low-key voice. I could tell she was wearing out, and I was glad.

"You made my point for me. Making money is the only game in town for these business people," he retorted, energized like a boxer who has his opponent on the ropes.

"How do you think jobs are created, anyway? It's from profitable businesses," she said, "that make things or provide services that people want to pay for."

"A major role of government is to create jobs," Keith interjected.

"Look, in every presidential election in this country for the last forty years," Sonia replied, "the Dems talk about creating jobs, as if they have any clue what they would actually do about it. But the government creates payrolls, not real, sustainable jobs. Those come from profitable companies that create and satisfy demand. I think you have been in the educational ivory tower too long, professor."

"Listen, young lady, every PhD faculty member at my university, and at others around the country, agrees with me about the government creating jobs. It is not disputable." He smiled slightly as he delivered the low blow, effectively saying, "We are smarter than you."

"Yeah, and the reason there is so much solidarity is that unless a professor adopts this narrow, unrealistic ideology, he or she will never have a permanent position. I saw a study that said the political science department at UC Berkeley is only eleven percent Republican, and it's only slightly better at Stanford. Are kids getting an education or an indoctrination? Even the liberal-leaning students," Sonia blasted, "can't debate the topics 'cause there's no one who disagrees with them, or nobody who will admit it."

"If it's the right way to think, that doesn't make it bad, but—"

The low clouds lit up as a sharp thunderclap stopped Keith in midsentence. The cracking blast shook the ground and opened up a downpour of cold, driving rain. Sonia pulled her collar around her neck and flipped the hood over her head. She leaped off the rock with both feet landing on the ground at the same time, but her right foot took a step around the rock, and by the time her left foot and the rest of her body caught up, she had vanished into the black night. Keith and I moved quickly toward the tents but at the pace of middle-aged men with more to move and less agility to propel us. There was no camaraderie or acknowledgement between us about our declining mobility. No nodding. No winks. It was raining too hard. We just ran.

6

The rain pounded on the tent walls and seemed to wash away the contentious campfire debate from my mind. I crawled into the sleeping bag fully clothed, shifted down until it covered my cold, shivering shoulders. Slowly, thoughts of last summer jumped into my head. I was in Jamaica, a last-minute trip by myself just to get away from the city. What a different place than this riverbank, hot and lush from twelve months of rain, but the most striking difference is that the people are so poor in Jamaica. Outside the rain fell harder. I looked up into the pitch-black tent, which gave no suggestion of my whereabouts as I felt my body gradually relax, my eyes close. I fell into a deep sleep.

"Pick a spot on that rock and stare at it. You might stay balanced if you keep your eyes focused. Try lifting the right foot; dip it in the mini-pool of rushing water. Fast. Dry your bare foot with the towel, stick it in the sandal quickly before you fall over," I said to myself, lean-ing and shaky. "Keep your eye on that spot, on the rock, on one foot, in the water."

Both sandals on my feet, dry, no sand, pretty good. The wa-ter was refreshing but not too cool, about eighty degrees. The pool caught and accumulated the water from the falls. Handmade, head-size rocks stacked and capped off with bags of small stones formed a dam to hold the water. Through a thumb-size hole in the top of one of the bags, I could see the stones were a variety of colors with edges rounded by thousands of years of work from the hand of God. The bathers crawled over the top of the bags into the waist-high pool. They were flailing, frolicking, and splashing. About three at a time fit under the falls as it plunged a modest thirty feet onto the heads and shoulders of the swimmers. The pounding on their heads was the price they were paying for the massage on their shoulders. The winding riverbed below was draining the tiny water flow through the last miles of the Blue Mountains into the warm Caribbean Sea.

I lifted my head and pulled myself up onto my right elbow. Reaching with my left hand, I found the tent wall. "I'm on the river, dreaming about Jamaica," I said to myself as my heavy eyelids, in the darkness, collapsed into sleep and my head found the makeshift pillow on the tent floor.

"Hey, mon, you buy some mangos, two hundred J," he shouted as he strolled in my direction. Next to the fruit stand there was a shack made of corrugated tin, indistinguishable from the hundreds of others all over Jamaica. A contraption that looked like a combination of a chicken cage, a vegetable strainer, a violin bow, and an ice cream maker with a crank handle sat in a little, red Flexible Flyer wagon without much red remaining on the weather-beaten wood.

"Not today. How did you make this?" I asked as I pointed to the fantastic machine. I thought to ask what it did or who it did it to, but stopped short.

A quiet, bored, and slightly unsettled look migrated onto his face as he quietly uttered, "Turn-hand-make-fashion."

My blank stare did not catch him by surprise. Even though a simple roadside warrior, he seemed accustomed to talking to "whites." My eye wandered to the dry riverbed behind the tin shack. The scorched sand and rocks shrugged off the broken-bottle-tin-can population covering it, and it looked fresh and vibrant and decades old at the same time. The array of debris, old and new, was not litter or trash. It lay there as a necessary part of the environment, part of now, part of my mango seller's life. Even if somebody tried to clean it up, the littered riverbed wouldn't go away. The litter would reappear. It belonged there.

"You take what you got and make what you want," he said, explaining himself.

The late-night TV blared the news. From slits in my eyelids, I could see her behind the news desk, nice-looking bouncy blonde, like all the other blondes. "Half the marriages in the U.S. end in divorce. It's because the river is too deep, it's too wide, it's too cold, it's too hot, it's too clean, it's too dirty. The river is too vast. There is too much potential, and the handbook is out of print. When the music stops, do you have a chair? Get your chair early and marry your high school sweetheart. Get her quick before she disappears. There is a two-for-one sale at Wal-Mart on the fourth of July, no handbook required."

I rolled over in my sleeping bag, opening one eye at a time, and looked at the top of the tent just three feet above my head. The faint light of the morning sun shone through the waterproof fabric that looked almost dry from the inside. The rain had stopped for now. The only sound was the steady drone of the river. Then the whole tent started shaking.

"Get that fishing pole, buddy. Let's catch some breakfast."

I crawled out with my fishing rod and the small box of flies I bought from the hole-in-the-wall fly shop on Union Street in San Francisco.

"Where's the coffee, Davy?" I tossed out.

"Davy?" Mike said.

"Davy Crockett. Get with the program," I said while straightening my rain parka.

"Oh yeah, Davy Crockett," he replied. "Anyway, coffee is for wimps, and you won't need those flies."

"Okay, we're going to catch them with our hands, right?" I said.

"That's how I usually do it, but in case that doesn't work, I bought these local flies in the sports shop in Salmon next to the motel. Local caddis and even fat nymphs if we can't talk them into rising," he said.

"I was counting on that. Did you bring the tarter sauce?" I replied.

"Tarter sauce is for wi—"

"I know, is for wimps," I said.

We walked downstream along the riverbank for a few hundred yards until Mike found an eddy in the river and positioned himself near a steep overhang on the bank that looked like a hiding place for wild trout. I watched the fast-moving water from the middle of the river curl back to the right and flow upstream in a circular movement to form the eddy, settling on a spot where the riverbank jutted five feet out at the lower end. A little cover under the overhang, deep enough to keep it cold, close to the fast water for food supply and relief from the current. A few small riffles formed on the side of the eddy where caddis, nymphs, and other food fall out of the river flow. Big trout can rest there from the current and feed easily. Good fishing here.

I pulled my rod out of the hard-shell case and slid the reel onto it just above the cork handle. Tying a caddis fly on the end of the leader line, I squeezed out a drop of floatation liquid onto my forefinger and thumb and stroked the artificial bait, careful not to spear my skin with the razor-sharp barb. I whipped the rod a few times in the air to draw out the line and then let it fall into the water upstream from the targeted overhang. I whipped the rod tip again to mend the feeder line upstream, assuring the fly would float down at the natural speed of the current and waited as the slow current of the eddy moved the fly into range of the rising fish. Looking across the river, I saw the early-morning light cut through the narrow canyon and gently layer itself on the crystal water. The reflection of the red sun and the cotton sky painted a color pallet on the water canvass of yellow, orange, and purple. This was the third day, the buzz had vacated my ears, and my liberation from civilization was all but assured. Then the muffled sound of voices penetrated my quiet conversation with the river.

"…they're not easy to catch. It looks like it's about the rod and the reel and the flies, but it's not. It's more about a quiet mind. A quiet mind allows you to be part of nature. You have to be still to understand how to be part of nature," Mike was explaining.

Sonia said in a respectfully low voice, "Nature isn't all that benign, Mike. Survival is a struggle for all species."

It looked like Sonia had run into Mike while taking an early-morning stroll.

"What I mean," Mike continued, "is that you can't skate off the information super highway onto the back roads of the wilderness and catch a fish with a fly rod. You have to take the time to relearn things. There has to be a rebirthing in your mind to get in sync with nature."

"Well, I appreciate the Zen of it all, but we are here and we are eating food from the supermarket and drinking the beer you guys brought and sleeping in tents that came from Sports Mart. None of this is exactly spun from nature. I guess cell phones don't work out here, but the information highway is right around the next bend," Sonia replied.

"Yeah, but I'm talking about catching a fish with a fly rod. This part of nature has its own scale, its own rhythm. You can't be part of the workaday world and expect to be one with an ecosystem as intimate as this one. There is a group of organisms that live to reproduce once and die. The mayfly is one of these animals. Its larvae are deposited on the bottom of a river. The nymph forms and moves to the mid-depths. At this stage it is known as a midge. As it reaches the surface, it is called a cadis or mayfly. It looks like the mayfly lands on the water, but it actually just floats to the top. Then to dry its wings, it flaps them frantically in the air. This movement drives the trout crazy, and it can lead to a feeding frenzy. After it leaves the water's surface, the fly will mate in midair and drop back to the water, again attracting the trout. It all happens in a short period of time, and the fish feed on them during every stage."

Sonia was sitting on a stump about five feet from Mike. Her eyes followed the movement of his fly rod as his right arm heaved the pole over his shoulder. The fly whipped back at the end of the leader line once, twice, three times and onto the river. Each time more line pulled out of the reel, his casting motion slowed, but the exaggerated movement threw more line out from the rod each time, extending the reach of the bait. The artificial, brown, fuzzy food floated with the slow current into the feeding area.

Finally Sonia asked, "Are you at one with the fish or the fly?"

"There is always a point in nature when you don't hear a sound, a short time when you are sitting and the birds don't chirp and the wind doesn't rustle the trees. That's a window into nature. The silences in nature are the doorways into a secret world," Mike said, and after a moment he answered, "Both."

Mike always seemed so happy-go-lucky, but there was a quiet depth to him that he rarely revealed. He caught three sizable fish and carefully put each one back in the river. I had one strike from a monster rainbow, but he stripped the barb-less hook and got away. Sonia resumed her hike, and Mike and I meandered back to camp.

"What's the deal on Sonia?" I asked. "She was drawing some blood last night around the campfire."

"She's a cute little package. Knows her mind," Mike replied. "She could be a hard one to handle, especially if your politics are wrong."

The conversation dropped off as we walked toward the camp. The morning sun peaked through a broken cloud cover, taking the edge off the crisp morning air. The soggy, rain-drenched grass just off the path rustled from the movement of some brand of crawling resident, but neither Mike nor I reacted. We just walked quietly. Finally, Mike broke the silence.

"You ought to try to get to know her. It's time you hooked up with somebody to take your mind off that lousy golf game of yours."

"Yeah, well, I banked the six bucks last time we played, Mr. Cool," I answered. "I could get a crush on her if I tried. What do you think? Think it'd be child molesting?" I queried with a joke but hoping he would take the inference seriously and give me some advice.

"She's younger, but there's no child inside that skin. I think you should go slow and see if there's any meeting of the minds. That's 'minds,' buddy-boy, keep the other parts out of it for now," Mike cautioned.

"So you don't think the Conan the Barbarian technique will work with her?"

"You're lame with women, as usual, Conan."

1

The rain started a slow, steady drizzle as we tried to finish breakfast. I quickly abandoned the open-air dining hall and crawled in my tent, laid on my stomach, and planted my elbows symmetrically in front of me, giving my forearms and hands free movement. I then ungracefully cleaned my plate. Just then a booming voice shouted out directions.

"Listen up, everybody. It's a wet one, so roll those sleeping bags up, stuff 'em in your dry-bag inside your tent. Try to keep it all dry. Today is a good day for the paddle jackets, and wet suits can be picked up at the supply boat if you want one. This is a day that will put hair on your chests, boys. And yes, women, it will put hair on your chests too. Ooh, I just get the shivers when I talk dirty." Derek paused for a few seconds to admire his levity. "Remember," he said with the authority of a seasoned leader, "it doesn't do any good to fall in. You get just as wet on top of the river today."

I finished my packing and slipped through the narrow tent opening. The rain was falling lightly, and the low cloud cover was blocking any direct view of the sun. I looked toward Sonia's tent to see how she was managing her gear in the rain. I also wanted to gauge her reaction to Derek's crass joke, but she wasn't outside yet.

I walked around to the back of my tent and loosened the two metal stakes I had driven into the sand. They held well last night even in the face of some strong gusts. I looked up to see Sonia's dry-bag fly out of her tent. It hit the soggy sand and rolled over once before settling in a small puddle.

She stepped out, looked over her shoulder at me, and said, "Let's get these tents down to the boats. Come on, let's do yours first."

I threw the stakes on the sand beside my tent and folded the top onto the side as evenly as I could. Sonia took the front of the tent and lifted it up while I lifted the back. We folded the right side and then the left into the center. She bent the front into two-foot lengths toward the back, careful to brush the sand off as she went. We took down her tent, and she grabbed both and took off to the supply boat before I could offer to help. The rain slacked off as I picked up our dry-bags and looked at the kayaks lined up in a neat row on the beach. Sonia trotted back up the hill, and I held out her bag for her to take as we walked down to the water.

"Were you okay with Derek's comment this morning?" I asked.

"About the rain?" she asked with a questioning look.

"About the hair on the chest," I clarified.

"You're not one of those, are you?" she quipped.

"One of what?"

"One of those politically correct Nazi types?" she answered.

"No, nothing like that. But a lot of women would like to see gender differences left out of the conversation, especially with sexual overtones. They feel it degrades them."

Sonia took a deep breath as a gentle wind blew up the river canyon cooling the beads of rain on my face. I shifted the strap of my dry-bag up higher on my shoulder and straightened my back to accommodate the added weight. Sonia moved her left arm across her body and took the handle of her bag, lifting it from her right shoulder and, in a single motion, letting it drop in front of her. She stopped and turned to me with the most gentle, almost compassionate look I had seen from her in the three days I had known her. The weight of her body settled back on her heels as she began to explain her message, almost like a teacher showing a young student how to simplify a complex problem.

"People who don't live in the cities sometimes don't know about all this PC stuff. They live a simpler life where relationships are not as complicated and based more on what they need to do rather than somebody's idea of the way things ought to be. Derek didn't mean anything derogatory; he was just trying to lighten up a tense situation. The dry, river-guide-instructional-version explaining a bumpy morning coming up doesn't always resonate with people or keep their attention. It's like advertising. If you don't say things in a new, creative way, your message will get lost in the crowded fray. This is going to be a rough day on the river, and if we see signs of flooding, it could get hairy in these lightweight kayaks. I think a little color in the explanation helps to paint a picture of what we need to be thinking about this morning on this rough river."

"Well, sometimes the sexual innuendos can seem awkward and unnecessary," I said.

"I understand what you mean, and I support the whole women's movement. Women have many more opportunities and are taken more seriously in business and the workplace. Half of my friends played sports on college teams that didn't exist twenty years ago. But that doesn't mean I want to strip the spice out of life. Look, every reference to gender or sex is not an attack. It's fun to spar."

"Tell that to the women in the Bay Area," I said.

"I know women who go around scripting everybody's language," she continued, "and when people don't say things and do things the way they want, they get upset and try to say society is going down the tubes or that the guy is a pig. These women have a flat world, no color and no humor, and I think mostly they're insecure as people. Derek is not my type, but he's a fun guy, and we may need all the humor we can get today."

The boats were lined up on the beach, and I found one next to Mike. Sonia really made me think about things in a different way. She was far from helpless and not feminine in the "girly" sense, but her confidence and outdoorsy look made her drop-dead beautiful again this morning. So Derek wasn't her type? Yeah, well, that age was her type. Forget it, I thought. Then I looked up and saw Mike staring at me.

"You bagged out early from the campfire last night," I said nervously. It was the first thing that jumped into my head, and I hoped he hadn't noticed my wistful look.

"Well, I had to get my beauty sleep," he replied while stuffing his gear bag. He knew just what I was thinking but was letting me off the hook like a good buddy does every now and then.

"Yeah, well, as I said, Keith and Sonia went at the politics pretty hard. I was squirming a little bit," I said, trying to keep a little banter going while tying my own gear down.

A gust of wind blew a rolling ripple across the flat river. I dropped the straps I was holding, and my flat palms instinctively pressed down on the bag to hold it onto the boat while I waited for the water to level out.

"Well, Sonia won't last long in the ring with Keith in the long run," he said. "He knows his stuff. I've seen him disarm a lot of conservatives, a lot who thought they were up on the issues. Maybe she'll forget about your enduring devotion and fall in love with him," he said. "That would save us the misery of an ugly debate every night."

I felt my whole body tighten with a tense jolt. Conan the Barbarian was not happy with that little quip.

8

Mike shoved off from the shore and fell in behind the group. I walked out until the water lapped just below my knees, threw myself into the seat of the boat, and with two firm strokes on the right pointed the bow upstream into the swift current. The downstream flow caught the front of the boat, turned it abruptly to the right, and into the current. One stroke on the left straightened the craft, and I fell in line behind Mike.

The current was faster than yesterday. Small branches and other debris aimlessly floated along with us. The river bent to the left, and as I cleared the turn, I saw the boats crowding around Derek near the left bank. Approaching the group, I back paddled on the left and the boat slowed and turned toward the bank and the group. The rain had let up, and the surface of the river was smooth and flat.

Derek started, "Okay, this was a class two yesterday, but it's a class three today. If it keeps raining, it'll be a class five tomorrow, so let's get through this baby now."

Sonia smirked and said in a low voice, "Class five. Come on."

"I thought he was a fun kind of guy," I whispered with a subtle smile.

"Yeah, but class five?" she replied.

"There's a big hole in the middle," he continued, "but you have to hit it from the right side. So, run the rapid down the left bank. Just before that big rock, turn hard right and paddle toward the mouth of the wave. That hard right stroke will turn your boat left, and you'll hit the wave straight on. When— check that—if you fall out, let go of your paddle and float feet first. The guides will pick you up. Single file and follow me." Derek finished his instructions and turned toward the fast-moving water.

"This is going to be carnage no matter what class it is," Sonia whispered.

Keith paddled hard to get behind Derek and in front of Simon. I watched as Derek hit the hole, his boat disappearing for an instant as the bow nose-dived into the crevice. Then suddenly, his yellow craft shot up in almost vertical flight. His bow pierced the front of the wave, and reaching forward, he dug his paddle into the face of the curl and pulled back with a fierce motion, causing his boat to blast through to the other side. He turned hard right and settled his boat in a small, tenuous eddy, waiting to help fish out the would-be swimmers. Keith followed and, as he made it through the wave, headed straight downstream following the current and right past Derek. Mike was next while Sonia, Simon, and I waited at the top of the rapid.

Sonia floated up to Simon and said gently, "Stay right behind me and instead of a hard right stroke before the hole, give it a nice easy back paddle on the left. That should turn you into the wave just fine. Are you all set?"

Simon gave her a slight nod and said, "Let's go."

He stayed two boat lengths behind her and mirrored her every move. Just before the hole, he dipped his paddle in on the left side and gave the effortless back stroke, as instructed.

The boat jutted left into the soft flow of the hole, and as his bow hit the wave, his long arms reached forward to the front of the boat and, with a massive stoke, thrust the craft through the wave. He accelerated past Derek, raised his paddle above his head with both hands, and let out a piercing yell. Sonia grinned from ear to ear. When Mike and I made it down, Simon raised his paddle again, and the whole crew, knowing they beat the river, raised their paddles and gave a jubilant cry.

We ran a succession of three rapids with no major hurdles, and then the water flattened out and we leisurely floated down with the current. The boats spread apart almost in single file, and the whole crew seemed to be enjoying the rest and solitude of an easy float down the river. When the sun peeked out through the clouds, I could feel the warmth penetrating my paddle jacket.

I heard a swoosh of water and then, "You jerk," and something big slapped onto the water's surface.

"You're going to pay, I swear, you *are* going to pay," I heard from behind me.

"Let the games begin," Simon shouted.

I looked back to see Derek sculling his boat in wide circles around a swimming Sonia. She was holding on to the sides of her kayak as her floatation vest held her shoulders and head above the water level. He moved closer and tried to hand her paddle back to her in a tentative gesture. When her fingers touched the paddle, she grabbed the blade and jerked it toward her, trying to snare her opponent. Derek quickly let go of his blade end, and the paddle dropped to the water as Sonia thrust herself toward his boat. Her hand fell on the right gunnel, and she closed her fingers, trying to get a grip on his craft. Derek's wide grin vanished for a split second as he dipped his paddle into the water on the left. His easy back paddle pulled the boat away, and Sonia's hand dropped into the water. Derek's grin reemerged while Sonia's wide smile betrayed her seeming anger. She had been ambushed and thrown into the water, beaten in a playful competition that she didn't know was coming, but she was having a ball. There they go again, I thought. The young crowd.

Derek floated by me, moving to the front of the pack when Keith shouted out, "Picking on the girls? Going for the easy targets, I see."

Keith was trying to be part of the fun, and that friendly gesture would likely get him into the fray. But he had little chance to win a water battle with any of the guides. They spent four months a year on the river paddling these kayaks. The strength in their arms and shoulders allowed them to effortlessly maneuver these boats around.

"I can flip that guy like a matchstick. Girls are easy targets, my ass!" Sonia said as she floated alongside Mike and me. She looked in good humor but defiant, like a young horse kicking loose a new saddle, refusing to be broken, determined to keep the rider on his own feet and not on its back. I could see the exuberance of youth in Sonia. Somehow she couldn't focus on defeat. Whatever the odds, and they were huge, she only saw herself winning this contest.

River jousting is a huge favorite with kayakers, where competitors stand in their boats and jab at their opponents, trying to knock them off balance. Derek had instigated a surprise attack on Sonia, floating up stealthily behind her, attaining a firm hold on the back of her craft before flipping it and Sonia into the drink. He was a master practitioner of that move, and although she felt the need and the innate ability to dump him in retaliation, she stood little chance of succeeding.

"I see Derek is spreading the humor a little bit, Sonia. What a guy," I said.

"He'll pay for his indiscretions. That grin will fade to blue, just wait," said the wild horse.

Keith spread his feet to the edges of his boat, wedged them in, and stood straight up, though tenuously, preparing to challenge would-be attackers, but his rudderless kayak quietly entered a small twist in the current and spun end-to-end. With only the river current propelling them, the other boats floated downstream, leaving Keith and his challenge unanswered. His boat wobbled, and close to losing his balance and collapsing into the water, he managed to sit back down without falling in, but several hundred yards behind the group.

We continued to float leisurely down the wide, slow stretch of river. I caught up with Mike, and he looked over and said, "Maybe she won't be falling in love with either of those guys very soon."

"Give it time," I said. "Good things take time, Mikey."

I felt my stomach churn a little bit as I spoke the words. A woman like Sonia calls her own shots; she does what she wants and lets the chips fall where they will. So I needed to back off and just watch. Keep my expectations low. Fantasies—those are what get you, I thought. You start thinking out ahead of yourself and start dreaming of what it might be like, and then the reality never matches the vision. Well, it wasn't that bad, but I would just back off. That's what I would do. After all, this was day three, the office was far away, and all I had to worry about was getting down the next rapid.

Sonia and Simon floated up and caught up with me, and the three of us steadily and meticulously paddled our way down the flat stretch of water. Nobody spoke for what seemed like ten or fifteen minutes. A group of four egrets flew lazily overhead, their wings spread wide and fixed in a majestic glide while surveying the river's path from above.

I wanted to get some conversation going with Sonia, but nothing seemed right to say. A few quips about how she got dumped in the water by Derek? Wrong. What about Alicia's tennis accident? No good. How about those burgers last night? I couldn't think of a thing. Maybe the women's thing from this morning. She loved to argue political stuff.

I let the lazy river current carry us down for a few more minutes. Finally, I looked over at Sonia and said, "Maybe this women's PC thing is kind of like a spiritual fad?"

When I said it, I bit my lower lip in shame. What was I doing making silly conversation about politically correct stuff?

She considered for a moment before answering, her arms moving in slow, rhythmic strokes. "Spiritual might be a little generous, but social causes do take on a religious zeal, I think. The problem is that religious zeal takes on a life of its own. The point here is that even when the facts change or are better known, the argument stays the same. In other words, the zeal is fixed in time because it's more of a feeling than a reality." She paused again as we floated slowly down the river. "I hope I'm not coming across too preachy, but this is why these arguments about social issues, environmental causes, and so on, get emotional and breed personal attacks. It's because solving the problem becomes secondary to the religious zeal. And make no mistake, it goes all the way from the far right to the far left."

"Kind of takes on a life of its own," I interjected. "I have to say, I never have taken time to think about it that carefully, but I can see what you're saying."

"Yeah, a life of its own," she said almost under her breath. "It's like the Vietnam War. Do you know much about that nasty little episode?"

"Well, if being in it counts, I guess I know a little about it. Didn't see combat, though. After it was over, I went to grad school and wanted to get past it as soon as I could," I answered.

"The dirty truth is that the facts got lost and the thing took on a life of its own."

"Come on, there were some good reasons to do what we did," I protested.

"Here's the way it went down. President Kennedy faced a hostile cold war environment with the Soviet Union literally pounding shoes on the table to proclaim they were going to bury us, while this whole insane nuclear arms race raged on."

"Right. In high school we practiced bombing drills," I said.

"I'll bet you don't forget that."

"No, you don't," I answered.

"While the Soviets were trying to convert other countries to communism, we developed the idea called the domino theory, which was that if one country fell to the commies, they all would. So stopping the fall in Vietnam was part of the game. The Kennedy team never planned a war and certainly didn't want to move in U.S. troops because they never, for a second, thought we could win a war in that environment. Then Kennedy was shot and the new group took over under President Johnson. As the generals and bureaucrats rotated in and out, the institutional memory of the original concept was lost and the mantle of war was taken up by a new more zealous group each time."

"I don't remember—why didn't Johnson step in to hold these gung-ho guys back?" I asked.

"That was the sad part. Johnson did a political trade with the war hawks in Congress. If they voted for his War on Poverty programs, he would push the Vietnam War forward. It worked great for those guys, but it was a bad deal for everyone else."

"Then President Nixon came along."

"Nixon entered office with a war-torn electorate and a failing conflict in Southeast Asia. He found a way to end the whole thing within a couple of years, thank God."

"I guess that really did take on its own life," I concluded.

"Yup, it did, but that's what happens all over. I see it in businesses I cover for my magazine all the time. A company is serving customers best, for example, by using a particular process or structure, then the customer changes, the product changes, or the competition changes and the people don't notice because they weren't trained to serve the customer, they were trained to be in the process."

"This 'life of its own' thing is really big," I said, stretching out the last words and drawing both arms up in a big circle around my head, taking a risk by making fun of her, but three days was up and I wasn't going to get too serious about anything. Just then we floated into a small rapid, really more of a ripple, which nevertheless caused me to sit up and wedge my bare feet into the folds on the floor of the boat to stabilize myself from the rocking motion. Just to the left, the other boats headed for a small sandbar on the bank with a rock face jutting up more than thirty feet from the river level, where we beached for lunch.

The sand area was no more than fifteen feet from river to rock face, which gave the guides only the minimum space they needed to set up the lunch table. They moved like a well-oiled machine, unpacking, setting up, and getting ready to spread the food out. Derek showed Mike a path up through the jagged rock face that led to a natural hot spring. River outfitters had carried cement up the steep path and used loose boulders to build a small dam that formed the pool. The edges of the cement were rounded and smoothed by many seasons of sun, wind, and rain. I stood above the crudely built pool and looked down at the random rocks and oddly placed cement. There was no design, just first come, first serve. If a big rock got there first, it went into the wall. If a bag of cement came next, it got poured. Random and crude, haphazard and loose, it was a perfect pool for part-time river rats like us. We were up high enough to see several bends in the river from our morning run, and every section we could see was tainted with brownish, murky runoff from the heavy rain.

I jumped from rock to rock until I was in front of the pool and had nowhere to go but in, then slowly immersed a foot, an ankle, a leg, then two legs, and voila, the hot water was tickling the bottom of my chin.

The others followed, and the pool almost felt crowded when Sonia's head peeked over the rock's edge from the trail below.

"Get a move on it. This hot water may run out soon," Simon blurted out in Sonia's direction.

Of course, the hot spring was like the river. It was there before we existed, and it would be there after we were gone. Simon liked to be a cutup, and I could tell he was feeling very gracious toward Sonia for her help on the river. He loved the adventure of this sport, but it looked like his river skills were not as robust as his enthusiasm. Sonia was humble and didn't appear to need acknowledgement or even thanks.

She grinned at Simon's remarks and muffled a short reply that I didn't hear. Reaching the top of the trail, she stopped for a breath after the steep climb, turned away from us toward the river, and looked up the canyon for a moment at our morning traverse and winding descent. Keith and Mike were comparing personal notes on their river skills that helped them conquer the rapids while Simon was studying the dam construction quietly and meticulously. Sonia stood on the top of the rock face, reached to her waist, and slowly pulled her river shirt up over her head. The skin on her tanned waist and back were only cloaked by a thin bikini strap. She let the shirt fall to the rock at her feet and carefully unbuttoned her shorts. With a wiggle, her shorts dropped to her feet. Light broke through the battered branches of an old tree from overhead, which filtered the glare from the noonday sun. The small of her back formed a delicate line down to her narrow waist, which gave way to a bikini, only slightly covering a perfectly rounded bottom. While Keith and Simon talked about the rapids, my eyes stayed fixed on Sonia. The uneven sunlight gave her sandy hair a curious tint of redish-orange as she lowered her body toward her rock perch. The low rumble of the river was the only sound I could hear, and Sonia was the only thing I could see. She took the few steps to the pool and slowly immersed in the warm water.

"Okay, let's get it before the flies do," Derek yelled up from the sandy beach below.

Keith and Simon lined up first for lunch, each piling a paper plate high with sliced ham, turkey, Swiss cheese, tomatoes, and pickles. Potato salad came from a quart-size plastic jar, and a can of soda topped off the meal. It takes more fuel to paddle the rapids than to sit at a desk, and my plate was piled high with the same mound of calories as the rest. I found a semi-flat rock to sit on near Mike and set my root beer next to me on the sand. As the plates emptied, Simon started to chat about his trip to Alaska. I looked up to see the bank across the river, which was a five-foot wall of rock. The light gray limestone face was adorned with stripes of faded iron-red sheets horizontally layered into the rock face. As the river bed turned left, the water slammed straight into that bank, stripping it of any loose dirt or standing stones. The current bounced off this ribbon of rock and in a fizzling fury redirected itself down the center of the channel.

"No, we didn't want to take a cruise," Simon was saying. "We wanted to explore the interior and get a feel for the lifestyle, just take a look at what people do in that part of the world."

"So you got off the coast and into the backcountry? Did you see any drilling rigs?" Keith asked.

"Not that I recall, and not that much backcountry, really. We did take a two-hour plane ride over the tundra and backcountry, but I'm telling you that single-engine plane scared my wife to death. We hit a thermal pocket on our way back to the Sitka airport, and it felt like the whole plane dropped fifty feet. The pilot just chuckled and said it happens almost every time he's up. But, Jesus Christ, it was scary," Simon said with a sigh.

"I'm a senior advisor to an organization that is desperately trying to keep drilling out of the Alaskan wilderness," Keith said matter-of-factly. "But it will be an uphill battle with the pressure from the big oil companies and the mood Washington is in for more oil at any cost to the environment."

Simon looked up from his plate with only a few bits of potato salad left on it. He nodded in a respectful manner to acknowledge that he was listening.

Keith continued, "Before this current administration in Washington, I felt we had serious momentum for environmental awareness, but in the last few years we have lost the big MO. The pristine wilderness has to be preserved for future generations. We've got to make it happen."

Simon's eyes panned the river canyon. Small, calm ripples lapped onto the sandy bank a few feet away. The canyon walls narrowed and disappeared as they wound through the valleys, channeling the river north. His eyes still fixed on the river, Simon opened his mouth and slowly spoke.

"It is really beautiful land." He paused. "The interaction of the ecology of an area like that, or the entire planet for that matter, is just beginning to be understood. I would guess that a hundred years from now we will know a great deal more about the interaction of all species and how they are interdependent. What is that thing about a butterfly flapping its wings in China and affecting the weather in California?"

"It's something like that," Keith said. "It's from a concept called chaos theory, built on the idea that things are interconnected and many patterns are similar in nature, though the time frame or size may be different."

Mike chimed in, "Simon, here's an example from my business. I can show you two stock charts that look very similar. The ups and downs are in the same places. The lengths of the troughs are just alike, yet one is from a stock's one-year price history and the other is from the last ten minutes of trading."

"But they look the same?" Simon asked.

"Yes, they call it a fractal. A big takeaway here is that things that may seem chaotic or random may be very ordered and have a structure that can only be recognized from a proper vantage point," Mike replied.

"Mikey boy, you are turning into a real philosopher. First it's the Zen of fishing and now chaos theory and world order," I said. "Will you be my guru?"

That got a laugh from everybody, even Mike. I looked right at him to bask in my successful dig, and he brought his right hand up to his grinning cheek, extended his middle finger, and began lightly scratching his nose. I couldn't help breaking into a huge grin. Yes, we were out on the river acting like school boys. The third day was the charm, and the buzz of civilization was out of my head. Let's go for more, I thought.

"But, Keith, are environmentalists against driving cars or having electric lights?" Simon asked, breaking off the revelry.

"Don't be silly. Energy production just needs to be accomplished without harming the environment."

"Whose environment?" Sonia interjected. "Maybe it's a bit chauvinistic to protect our pristine lands as long as some foreigners in some far-off place keep drilling and pumping the oil to run our turbines. What if there is a spill there? Who cares, right?"

"Of course we care. Ecology is a worldwide proposition," Keith replied.

"Well, where is the manual on that? Where are the journal articles to protect the pristine wilderness of Saudi Arabia? If you want fossil fuels, you have to drill and pump them. Yes, you have to pump it as cleanly as you can, but you have to take the responsibility to produce it," Sonia said.

"Look, little lady, these wilderness lands support many critical species, and if they are destroyed, it erodes our ecological balance. It is crucial that we do all we can to protect them. There are hundreds of species lost every year already," Keith countered.

"Well, how many species are there in the world?" I asked.

"Nobody really knows at this point," Keith answered.

"If you don't know how many species there are in the world, year to year, how do you know if more are being lost than created or discovered?" I asked. "There's no constant to measure the numbers against."

"There was a loose theory that more species were lost because of pollution and environmental problems," Sonia said, "but the press and the environmental movement successfully changed it to a fact somewhere along the way, a known fact by the general public that has no basis in actual evidence. Nice job, right, Keith?"

"Some of these things get a little ahead of themselves, but Simon gets it. Even though we know little about the interaction of all species, our long-term survival may depend on it," Keith said, somewhat hotly.

"Wouldn't you agree with that, Sonia?" Simon asked.

"I agree wholeheartedly, but what is with the hyperbole and deception? Why can't everybody just use the real facts and let's get the job done? Like energy policy. Somebody gets in front of the cameras and says we need an energy policy and the next day the environmental hype-artists are calling him a lunatic and enemy of the people," Sonia said.

Before Keith could answer, Mike broke into the conversation, "The newest oil refinery in the U.S. is more than twenty years old, and rusting refineries are being shut down by oil companies all the time. Look, I don't know much about the social or environmental side of this, but my clients pay me to know what is going on in the real world, and I can tell you that there is a chokehold on oil production while consumption is growing. All the big oil discoveries were made more than thirty years ago. And by the way, oil fields deplete…they run out of the gooey stuff."

Keith had a strange look on his face. Mike was his broker, and he relied on Mike to keep his money growing, but this "need more oil" line was contrary to his own usual argument on the impact of oil drilling. I guessed that he had given that speech many times to thousands of devotees.

Keith broke in: "There was a monster find in the Caspian Sea near Kazakhstan in 1999, so I think you're exaggerating."

"That one is tied up in squabbles and may never produce much," Sonia interjected.

"Look, there is oil all over the world yet to be discovered. Let's leave Alaska alone," Keith continued.

Keith appeared to be outnumbered, but I knew Mike would back off soon to preserve his professional relationship. But I felt goose bumps on my arm when Keith mentioned Alaska again. Sonia would not let that stand. Her point was clear that drilling was not the responsibility of other nations on other lands. It was our country's duty to take at least some control over production to try to meet our huge domestic consumption needs. Keith was stuck in the environmentalist rut. Was safe energy production their goal, or was no production their goal?

I decided to throw Keith a bone and introduce his area of expertise, global warming. I would rather have left this conversation to the rest of the group, and taken a walk, but the riverbank was vertical on either side of our beach. I had nowhere to walk except back up the hill to the hot spring, so I stayed. I was getting to feel like my "old self," but clearly they were feeling like their same-old-selves. The three-day rule might be a four-day rule for some in this group, but I was sure they would talk themselves out soon and settle into the beauty of the wilderness.

"Hey, Keith, how does this whole energy production issue relate to global warming?" I asked.

Simon was looking out at the river, and Mike was staring at his lunch, but nobody left the group. It was like watching the local six o'clock news. You really didn't want to watch it, but you couldn't turn it off for fear of missing something juicy. I could feel the silent tension as everybody waited for Keith's response. He did not disappoint them.

"In a nutshell, carbon dioxide emissions are at such levels that they are overwhelming the atmosphere and triggering a variety of responses that will likely lead to a rapid warming."

"So what is the global temperature up, one degree?" Sonia chimed in. "That's more likely a result of natural cycles."

"Well, Miss Investigator, investigate this," Keith blasted back. "The difference between our climate now and the last couple of ice ages was only a few degrees, somewhere between four and eight. Small increments of change in temperature can cause massive change in the environment."

"But these kinds of changes take a long time. This is a big planet," Sonia said. "Come on, Keith, maybe the place is warming, but don't go rabid on us."

"Well, there is more carbon in the atmosphere than ever recorded in history, and high carbon dioxide levels are always present during periods of higher global temperatures," he said.

"Nice try. But how far back can data be available?" she replied. "Eskimos didn't keep records."

"Yes, in a way, they did," he snapped. "Sample ice cores go back over six hundred thousand years. They have bubbles trapped in them that clearly reveal the makeup of the atmosphere during each period. Again, no recorded period in the past has had these present carbon dioxide levels."

"Correct me if I'm wrong," Sonia said, "but the greenhouse effect is a natural phenomenon. In addition to carbon dioxide, methane, nitrous oxide, and even water vapor are responsible for holding heat on the earth so humans can survive."

"That's right. The planet would be about sixty degrees cooler without this layer and uninhabitable by humans."

"So it's a natural thing, and it's good for all concerned," she said.

Keith was getting more agitated, and Sonia was circling him like a gnat on a hot summer day. She, as usual, was bold and knew some details, but nobody else had the facts to outright dispute him. I was always skeptical of the so-called experts because they often have a dog in the fight, a point to prove. But what's wrong with reducing carbon emissions even if it turns out it's not causing global warming? It is causing air pollution. China is belching so much smoke that people have to wear face masks around some cities. The big picture is that the world is reaching the end of the first industrial revolution, where the standard of living skyrockets because of industrialization, which rose on the back of machines that burn fossil fuels and pour smoke into the air. Maybe the second industrial revolution will bring different kinds of machines and fuels, I thought.

"Maybe it's a case of 'too much of a good thing,'" Mike said.

There was a brief moment of silence while Keith was trying to regain composure. He was pacing in a small circle with his hands clasped together while his face was blushing red. High-strung and packed full of details on this warming topic, he wasn't tolerating uninformed opposition well.

"I don't want to get too technical, especially for Sonia's sake," Keith snapped.

That got a chuckle from Simon, and it would have from me except that I was nurturing my infatuation with Sonia and held it back.

"There are these things known as feedback loops. They are self-feeding cycles that can accentuate a situation like a warming trend," Keith said with an air of expertise. "For example, as the ice melts, the hundreds of square miles of white surface that was reflecting light away is now a darker sea or land that absorbs light, turning it into heat, and this speeds up the warming. There are computer models for these feedbacks, but it is hard to know exactly how they'll function."

"Then how do you know these feedback loops will make any difference at all?" Sonia asked.

"We know they work 'cause we can see them in action," he said. "Look at the force of the last hurricanes to hit the Gulf of Mexico. Conditions are becoming ripe for extreme weather patterns."

"Here you go again," Sonia shot back. "A couple of big hurricanes don't prove the t-h-e-o-r-y of global warming," she said, elongating the word "theory" for emphasis. "Hurricanes have multi-year cycles. When you take a broad brush and paint everything 'global warming,' you lose your audience for a lot of this hype."

Keith's face was still red, and I could just feel the blood starting to boil in his veins. Sonia wasn't actually pushing the envelope, but she wasn't exactly endearing herself to the PhD from Irvine.

"There are a lot more severe storms reported now because parts of the world were ignored in the past," Sonia said. "Data was only collected for the areas that the developed countries cared about. Massive hurricanes were known to have happened in remote areas that never made it to the stat books, so naturally with these areas now added to the data, it looks like there is more activity."

Keith started to give his response when Derek gave the order to man the boats and get back on the river. Keith walked over to the trash can and slammed his paper plate into the plastic bucket, keeping his gaze fixed on the sand as he strode to the river's edge. I thought he was holding his own in these spats, but he appeared to be taking the battle a bit too personally. He'll shake it off, I thought.

9

Sonia wadded up her napkin, folded it inside her paper plate, slowly rose from the rock, and walked over to the lunch table. After tossing the paper into the five-gallon plastic trash bucket, she turned and dashed toward the water where Derek stood. He was facing the river and didn't see her flying toward him. Sonia's arms straightened in front of her, and when she reached Derek, she lowered her shoulder and threw her weight into her assault. With just enough force to lift him from his feet, her forward momentum thrust him toward the wide, slow river current. As he crashed into the water, he turned to see Sonia and the look of fear on his face turned to a wide grin. The momentum of Sonia's attack left her off balance and falling toward the water too. Derek twisted forward just enough to wrap his arms around Sonia. Just before they both disappeared under the river, he yelled with exuberant glee, "You're comin' in too."

It was payback time for Derek, and Sonia retaliated for the river soaking she got from him with an attack when he suspected it least.

After a moment, they popped up and swam the few strokes it took to get to knee-high water. To the cheers of everyone on the bank, they turned to each other, locked arms, and stepped onto the dry sand.

He took her right hand and raised her arm into the air, like a prizefighter, and said, "The winner."

We roared with approval, except for Keith, who was still pacing and red faced. I clapped with little enthusiasm because the sinking feeling in my stomach was migrating against gravity up into my throat at the sight of Sonia and the young buck.

Watching them play around, my thoughts digressed to a time when I was young and full of youthful exuberance. Karen and I used to go to Stinson Beach north of San Francisco on Sundays before the kids were born. It was too cold to swim, and sometimes the fog made it almost too frigid to be there at all, but the salt air and knocking around the tide pools brought us out again and again. It was free to goof around out there, and we didn't have any money for recreation back then. One afternoon, an artist friend of hers came with us. We were walking near the water, letting the waves lap on our bare feet when he pulled three soft, baseball-sized balls out of his jacket and started tossing them in the air nonchalantly. I thought that was the coolest thing I had ever seen. In a matter of ten minutes he had taught me to rotate those three balls in midair. That week I bought my own juggling balls and worked on my technique, tried it a parties, but never got as good as I wanted to be. What a quirky little thing to do. I hadn't thought of juggling in years.

There was a small crowd around Sonia and Derek as the action was recounted, blow by blow—the look on Derek's face, the element of surprise, the slap when they hit the water. What was I thinking? I couldn't have a crush on a thirty-four-year-old, I said to myself. What would the kids say? And, what did I need a crush for? I was doing just fine.

10

The first half mile after lunch was a leisurely float. I pulled up next to Derek, and we began talking about the trip and the river.

"What's coming up this afternoon?" I asked.

"A couple of class threes, but the water is unusually high and the obstacles may have changed since last week. It's normal throughout the summer, though. First part of June, when the water is high, a bunch of these fun curls are covered by high water, and by this time of year a lot of the big boulders poke up and the river gets what we call 'more technical'—more holes to run and more rocks to hit your head on. That storm in Montana may be catching up to us. When the water is high, this next rapid can run a little too fast for some people," he replied with a stern look.

"Hey, everybody is loosened up by now. We'll all be okay," I assured him. "That storm looks like it's passed through and gone anyway."

"Flash floods occur six to eight hours after the storm," he said quietly. "Stay close to Keith for the next two runs. I'll ask Mike to stay with Simon. Chili for dinner tonight."

"You think those guys are a problem?" I asked.

"Well, not a problem, just like that, but Simon is a bit top-heavy and tipsy, and I'm afraid he's losing a little confidence. You need to be loose and agile to float into some of these boogers. You know what they say, 'loose hips saves ships,'" he said.

"I never heard that one," I said and then paused. "You think Keith is all right?"

"He's got the skills and the poise to run this whole river, but he is anything but loose. Keep it to yourself, but Keith is a danger out here right now. He's getting snappy and combative, and he's getting a little testy about listening to directions—all a bad combination."

"We're going to be okay, right?" I asked.

"I have run it like this in the spring, but not with guests. Let's just say, everything needs to go just right and we'll be fine."

"Nice move on Derek, Sonia." Simon floated in voice range of Sonia's kayak. "You probably haven't seen the last of him on this, but he can take a defeat like a real man. By the way, I've been overhearing some of your discussions with Keith, and I agree with a lot of what you're saying. I think it's time people start getting practical about these problems like oil production. Keith has some good points, and I'm at the top of the list of those who want a clean environment, but sometimes those guys get to be one-trick ponies. I mean, they build an argument on some buzzword like 'pristine wilderness' or something. I think pristine wilderness is important, but so is managing complex world economies, don't you think?"

"Yeah, there are a lot of big-picture areas that politicians reduce to sound bites. The long-term challenge of managing a complex economy gets diminished to opposition bickering. But decisions affect people up and down the economic ladder for many years after they're made."

Simon paused, and both he and Sonia paddled along in the calm river current. Neither seemed in a rush to blurt out more on the topic.

"Look over on the bank." Simon pointed to the right with his paddle.

At the water's edge, a small black bear was slowly meandering under the partial cover of a group of scruffy-looking trees. The small, furry creature glanced up at the kayaks but was unfazed. Its front paws sunk down into the soft, wet mud as he lowered his mouth into the water for a long drink.

"I love this trip," Simon said quietly.

Sonia nodded and dipped her paddle into the quiet water flow—right, left, and right again. Simon stayed beside her, a few feet to her left, and for a moment the river was all there was. We floated quietly for a long time. After a while, the river widened and the banks receded. The current carried us down the middle of this wider channel directly into the afternoon sun. In a low, quiet, kind of fatherly way, Simon looked over to Sonia.

"You know, politics is always ugly business. Are you old enough to remember when President Reagan drastically cut taxes and increased defense spending and the federal budget deficit ballooned?" he asked.

"No, but I'm old enough to remember studying it in school. The newspapers and the political opposition skewered him for years," she replied.

"The result was that the Soviet Union, trying to compete in the arms race, imploded, ending the cold war without a shot.

The tax cuts produced the greatest economic prosperity since World War II. Twenty years later, the budget was in a huge surplus and the Congress was fighting over how to spend it."

"Do you think any of the Democrats sent Reagan a thank-you note?" Sonia quipped.

"I really doubt it. They just keep wanting to raise taxes. There were no lessons learned. One-trick ponies, I guess," Simon uttered with a slight giggle. "The surpluses disappeared after the terrorist attack, though."

"They went quick. The military and intelligence agencies had been neglected and demoralized by the Clinton team. It was going to take serious money no matter who was in charge after that," Sonia said.

"But back to this global warming thing for a second," he said. "I read that an average American family is supposed to produce fifty tons of carbon dioxide every year—including their share of the electric grid and commercial trucking and shipping and so on."

"Yeah, well, this 'attributing' thing is extremely soft data, and much of it is just serving their cause." She paused. "But, all in all, this carbon thing needs to be solved, I guess. I just hate it when these self-serving zealots regurgitate these phony numbers and browbeat the public."

"You may have to get over yourself on this warming thing," Simon said in his fatherly tone.

"Yeah, I know," she replied.

Simon's boat floated into a crosscurrent that pulled him toward the right bank. He paddled forward and worked his way back to the middle of the river where Sonia was quietly paddling downstream. As he joined her, the sounds of the wilderness were all that could be heard, orchestrating its slow, smooth concerto.

"I hated to leave Alicia at home when she was the one who invited me. I think she'll be all right, don't you?" Sonia said, breaking the silence.

"She took a hard fall, but everything will heal with time. Who would have thought of tennis as a contact sport, anyway?" Simon quipped. "I was a little surprised that you decided to come along anyway. I mean, you didn't know anybody but me, and we're just a bunch of old guys."

"Yeah, well, I had blocked it out on the calendar, and politics is a little slow right now, so this is an easy time to get away."

"No romantic, island getaways for you these days?"

"Romance left the building along with Elvis, I'm afraid," she replied.

"Where did it go?"

"I don't know—maybe he got tired of talking about politics? A great guy, but I suppose we are different kinds of people. What's a girl gonna do?" she said.

"Relationships only work with compromise on both sides, and there has to be commitment, like an ultimate goal both people can strive for. Early on, my marriage suffered from having no goal, just two people doing their own thing at the same time. When Alicia was born, we had an instant long-term focus. All the rest of it faded away, and life settled into a groove. We were a unit, finally. Kids aren't the only way to do it—sports, religion, or politics, they all can work."

"I have this fast-paced-tear-it-up lifestyle, and so did he," she said.

"Maybe you need somebody older?" Simon said.

"Or younger," she said.

"A boy toy?"

"An intriguing idea," she said with a giggle.

Simon raised his right hand and pointed to a spot high on the bank. "An eagle's nest on top of that tree," he said softly.

I was in earshot and looked up just in time to see a bald eagle spread its wings in a slow, horizontal trajectory and descend to its perch atop the tallest tree on the bank. They watched in silence as the eagle settled in, and finally Sonia looked down at Simon.

"I always say that I don't suffer fools well. It's kind of an edgy stance to be in all the time," she admitted.

"You could soften the edges a little and still be the same person you are," Simon replied.

They floated without talking, as if the river were speaking and they were attentively memorizing every word it articulated. The shallow ripples shouted while the deep water groaned, and it all uttered a quiet truth.

"Yeah, probably a little too edgy," she said.

11

I reached the group of kayaks huddled around Derek just before Sonia and Simon.

Derek began to give his instructions on the rapid coming up.

"I walked up and took a look at this one. It's a new run today because the high water has covered some of the old holes, but it's brought in a few bugaboos on the right and one of the rocks we never worry about is going to be a 'do not go there' spot, so listen up. Run the first wave straight down the middle. After that, your boat will want to move to the right into the big eddy, so after you break through the wave, paddle hard on the right and point your bow toward the left bank. That will set you up for the big hole that is next. Once you are through that, eddy-out on the left and wait for everybody to assemble. Remember"—he raised his voice for emphasis—"do not get caught in the eddy on the right. If you do, don't go down. Paddle upstream, stay in the eddy, and wait for a guide."

"What's the big deal about the eddy?" Keith blurted.

"The eddy is fine, but you do not want to run the right side of the river today, and that eddy will spin you into a huge plume of white water and drop you down onto the jagged boulders below it. We don't want to have to scrape you off those rocks. The water is a little higher than I like to run it with guests, so stay focused," he replied with a calm but stern voice. He was looking directly at Keith.

The bow of Derek's kayak nose-dived into the hole guarding the first wave, and then reversed vertically, shooting up and hitting the water wall perpendicularly. He dug his paddle into the swift current in front and pushed forward, back paddling his craft just to the edge of the warned-against eddy. He waited there ready to help the rest of us. Sonia followed, hitting the first wave at a perfect angle. She paddled hard right as instructed and just before the second wave dug her blade into the foamy water, causing her boat to jerk left just in time to hit the wave straight on. She easily floated into the designated eddy and waited.

Mike and I watched Keith hit the first wave with Simon close behind him. The wave slammed into the left side of his boat, which began to roll right. Keith was nearly pitched out, but then out of pure force of will, he leaned into the wave, leveled his paddle, and jabbed it into the curl. His kayak righted itself, and the bow punched through the wave. He made it through the rough part but came out shaky and off balance. As he hit the small ripples below, he pitched and rolled and, in a quick instant, capsized and was separated from his kayak, but both were safe in the quiet swirl of the eddy. Just to the right I could see Derek begin to paddle ferociously upstream, and then I saw Simon dip into the hole.

"Oh, shit!" Mike exclaimed.

The confusion on the water gave way to chaos, and as I floated in the calm water above the rapid, the action seemed to slow while my field of vision widened. I could see the three boats bobbing in and out of sight while the current surged alongside them, and I could feel the panic as Simon collapsed into the crevice, dropped his paddle while his boat was thrust into the swirling do-not-go-into eddy, and he turned a full circle, and then a half circle, and Derek was able to grab the paddle, and he fought the current and got close enough to shovel the paddle to Simon, who did another half turn and floated by Derek while the current took him straight for the white water plume, and when he hit it he was backward, and the thrust doubled the boat over and Simon was thrown into the fizzling liquid and disappeared.

"Let's get down there. It looks ugly," Mike yelled over the muffled roar of the river.

"What?" I vaguely remembered saying, not really hearing what he said.

"Hey, guy, are you all right?" he asked.

"Uh, I guess. Yeah, let's get down there," I said.

We both shot through the rapid and joined Sonia, whose view of the incident was largely obstructed. Keith was near shore pulling himself from the water, still holding his paddle while his boat floated aimlessly about a hundred yards downstream.

"Are you okay?" Mike shouted to Keith.

"Yeah, yeah, I'm okay. Just waterlogged."

"I need Mike over here now, quick, get a move on it!" Derek called from across the river.

The equipment raft, which had followed behind us, cascaded down the rapid, and Derek flagged it frantically. The oarsman back paddled hard on the right and executed a series of wide sweeps with the left oar. The raft swung to the river's edge about fifty yards downstream from Derek. Just beyond the supply raft was a yellow, flat shape, knocking against the shore. It was Simon's kayak, deflated, floating, ruined.

Derek shouted to the guides, "I need a four-inch bandage, and I need it now."

Then we saw him holding Simon up with his right arm wrapped around Simon's chest in the waist-high water moving to the bank. The water behind the rock was relatively calm. Derek's left hand pressed his own shirt onto Simon's forehead.

"He made it," I shouted, breathing a sigh of relief.

"What do you mean 'made it'?" Sonia exclaimed.

"Simon got tripped up and got sucked into those rocks," I answered.

"It wasn't my fault," Keith said from his tenuous perch on the steep, rugged shoreline. "I slowed up a little just before the hole, just wanted to get a better look at it. Simon was too close. He should have slowed up too, looked at it better. Look, don't blame me."

Keith looked shaken and worn out. His hair draped down wet and straight, covering both ears, his back hunched slightly just below his shoulders. Sonia shot a perplexed glance at me, and I knew what she was communicating.

"No way, there was nothing you could have done," I said, trying to appease Keith. "I have seen a lot of wrecks on the river. They just happen and you go on. He'll be fine. The guides know how to handle this."

"Stay put, I'll paddle down and get your boat. Everything's cool," Sonia shouted to Keith as she pointed her bow downstream toward the empty kayak.

Derek dropped his right knee onto the air-filled pontoon of the equipment raft while he bent over to grab Simon's arm. The other guides helped lift Simon into the raft. The water was waist high, and the ground emerged from the river at a sharp enough angle to prevent our leaving our boats to help. Simon settled into the makeshift seat the guides made for him on the raft. He was conscious, but he looked dazed and groggy. Simon's right hand held Derek's shirt to his forehead, and Derek slowly removed it while wrapping the surgical four-inch bandage around his head.

"Okay, let's get everybody over here. We're all right, and we're going to be just fine. Simon got a nasty gash on his forehead and looks like he has a concussion, but no bones are broken, so there you are," Derek said to the group of kayaks assembled around the big raft. "The river is running pretty high, and the next stretch is going to be a little testy. If you go out, remember to let go of your paddle and go down the river feet first to push off the rocks. We will pick you up as soon as possible. Just stay calm."

"Simon needs medical attention. We need to get back to civilization. It's clear we need to get off the river," Keith snapped. He was looking up and down the river as he spoke, a bit of terror in his eyes.

"No place to get off. We're in a stretch that is not accessible by any roads. The next eight miles we are on our own," Derek countered. "Let's stay focused on the river, and we'll be in front of a fireplace sipping single malt sooner than you think."

"That man needs a doctor. Jesus Christ, Derek, call in a helicopter," Keith demanded with a high-pitched urgency in his voice.

"Yeah, well…no place to land, professor. The river dug this gulley out over a couple million years, and it's deep and narrow. No, it's eight miles to the whiskey, boys and girls, down the river," Derek said with a soft but firm tone. "The river's rising 'cause of the rains, but I don't think we'll get any flash flooding. We'll know more when we get to the Middle Fork."

"What do you mean? I'm sick of the hocus-pocus. What will the Middle Fork tell us," blurted Keith.

"About six miles down, the middle joins the main fork. The headwaters of the middle are a lot closer to the runoff source, and its canyon is a lot deeper and narrower. If it's flooding now, the main will be flooding soon, and then we may have to go to higher ground for safety," Derek said.

"What do you mean, 'safe—'"

"Shut the hell up, Keith," Sonia interrupted and the group fell quiet. "We're doing what Derek says, and we are shutting up. Got it?"

12

We ran the next two rapids with no major problems. I went out at the bottom of the second one, and Sonia was drying out from a spill on the first. The clouds had parted and the sun was high overhead, warming us up quickly. I pulled out my plastic, wraparound sunglasses and flipped the Croakie over the top of my head. The next three miles had no rapids, but the flat water was running very fast. The leisurely paddle strokes of yesterday were replaced with measured right and left paddling. We stayed in the middle of the flow, all settling in, single file. The water had risen beyond its usual level and up into the tree line on the steep left bank. For a stretch, the right bank flattened out and the rushing water covered the ground in a brown, muddy soup. There wasn't much talking and no river "jabber" or joking or baiting, just floating and waiting. Simon was behind us on the equipment raft. It was much more stable than the kayaks, and the guides had the experience and know-how to navigate the river. The somber atmosphere carried over to the guides, though, and it was easy to tell that they were treating the river with the respect it deserved.

Derek moved to the right side of the river and found a quiet eddy to pull the frightened troops into. I executed a series of sweeps on my left side, and the boat nosed to the right. As

I reached the quiet water of the eddy, I dipped my paddle on the right and pushed forward. The back paddle motion swung my bow upstream, and I settled in with the flotilla of worn-out vacationers.

"Okay, everybody, listen up," Derek addressed the crowd.

Floating just behind me, Keith whispered, "Mike, we've got to get off this river. Simon's hurt, and these guides are amateurs."

"Hey, Keith, put a cork in it, man. We've got some work to do," Derek shouted over the drone of the river.

Keith slammed his paddle down on his kayak and looked up, his lips tightly pursed in a straight line across his mouth.

Derek continued, "Hey, here's the lay of the land. Simon had a tough fall and the river is running high, but we can get down this little honey just fine. There is a takeout about four miles or so from here, and the vans will be ready for us. Let's just run it down the middle, and with this flow we can do it in a couple of hours. Look, the good news is that the sun is up and the rain is over, and there is a lodge with showers and the best chili chef in Idaho, right near the takeout. Hey, you could have been bored on the beach in Maui. This is adventure! Everybody out, let's take a break."

The raft pulled in the eddy, and its air-filled pontoons bounced onto the bank. Sonia and I jumped out of our boats and stood waiting for the guide to throw a tie-down rope from the pontoon boat. She waded, ankle deep, into the water and caught the two-inch nylon rope with both hands as the coil unraveled in midair. She turned and tossed the end to me while holding the curled loop with her left hand. I walked it around a sturdy pine tree and began tying it off, holding the taut line with my left hand while my right hand began moving the end, over and under, tying two half hitches. Then I felt a warm touch on my hand. I turned and saw Sonia crouching next to me. Her hand stayed on mine, and she gave a slight squeeze. I remember smiling a little. She didn't smile or frown but looked directly at me. Her eyes widened, and I found myself engulfed in her stare. The split second turned into a lifetime, and I felt like I had known her forever, or actually that she had known me forever. What I thought, where I had been, and where I was going. Time stopped for me, and the river disappeared. As she pulled her hand away, her thumb stopped just below my palm and began to rub in a circular motion. She stopped and looked up at me in silence. Her index finger stroked the taut line of scar tissue that caught her attention. The injury was not visible except for a faint white line of skin at close inspection. Sonia softly massaged the half-inch stripe. Her eyes moved up, but her gaze went right through me.

A few years ago while playing a pickup game of basketball, a friendly match suddenly became extremely competitive, as they often do with boys of all ages. Jumping for rebounds off the backboard, three of us tangled our feet in midair, landing our collective weight like a drunken squid on hard, weather-torn asphalt. My knee hit the pitted surface first, opening up the skin to a slight, spontaneous spurt of red blood. My left hand went down next to catch the brunt of the fall from the slow descent of the snarling bodies. The rutted surface and the loose gravel ripped the flesh away from the palm of my hand in a two-inch, uneven radius. The wound took two months to heal, and the scabs slowly turned to a new layer of soft, white skin rutted in the mirror image of the weather-furrowed asphalt.

"Sports?" she said, half asking, half telling, and not expecting a reply.

Then she said, "I'll tie a bowline, it'll hold better."

She tied the mariner's knot with ease around the tree while I stood in silence.

Mike brought over an apple and a granola bar for each of us. Sonia took hers and turned to walk to the raft. Then she stopped, turned back around, and looked at me with a brief glance, then hopped on the raft, and began talking to Simon.

"This whole thing is a piece of cake," Mike said after Sonia left. "River is running a little high, but it's like this in the spring, anyway. A little testier, but that's part of the fun. Are you and Sonia getting a little friendly?"

"Naw, she's just helpful when she can be," I answered.

I felt light-headed with a slight flutter in my chest. She's interested? Maybe, maybe not. Kind of aggressive? Maybe, maybe not. She's a different type of girl. Don't push it, I thought, let things unfold.

I sat down to watch the river and thought about Jim's last two years in Singapore with JP Morgan, and Georgia with two more years at UCLA. Both of my kids had managed to grow up in good shape, and soon nobody would be left in the nest. Actually, they'd been almost-gone for years. I called both of them on their cell phones about every week, and I made sure Georgia had enough money for school, but our visits were few and far between. Raising independent, self-reliant, and most of all self-supporting kids was my goal, but for a while I felt a little abandoned once they were both out of the house. Jim would call, after staying under the radar for a month, and pick up the conversation like everything was the same as he left it.

He thought time stopped for me when he left and that things would always be the same. The funny thing was, they were much the same. I'd been the single parent for ten years, and that included all of Jim's high school time. I put together a routine that worked for everybody: soccer, plays, homework, and running a company. We all made it through with a certain amount of respect for each other. I had some opportunities with dating, but nobody seemed to fit in with the family or the job or our routine. I'm too picky; I could admit that. There is a certain amount of comfort, just being on your own, making up your own schedule, your own friends, not having to small talk, or go shopping for cute tops at the boutiques. If I wanted a quiet night, I got it, no questions asked. Of course, if I didn't want it quiet, sometimes I got it anyway.

13

The trees on the bank were firmly rooted, some in fertile soil while others rested precariously on hard, rock surfaces, sending roots down to wherever they could find a toehold against the harsh rain and wind. But these land-loving old salts on the bank were not accustomed to the current's persistent, high water force. The banks were striped of leaves, twigs, and small branches, all of it washed into the relentless flood downstream. I paddled around several clumps of tangled debris, pushing some of them away from my boat's vulnerable plastic sides. We ran through stretches of rapids that had virtually disappeared because the high water submerged the previously imperiling rocks, converting waves, curls, and holes into flat, fast water. The river did not run easily, though. The swift current could sweep you to either side of the river into logs or branches or newly formed eddies, isolating you from the group. Any mistakes were accentuated by the fast flow, and every person in the group was in high awareness. My heart racing, I could not relax; each paddle stroke was deliberate and measured to keep my craft in the right flow of the river, down the middle, following Derek, not thinking, just reacting to what might come my way. I caught up to Mike. He turned between strokes, cocked his head slightly, and showed his teeth in a wide smile. He saw it all in my face: grim and bleak and way too serious.

"You need to lighten up, buddy. It's best to stay loose," Mike admonished. "You'll do your best staying loose," he reiterated.

I looked ahead and saw Keith and Sonia. Keith was paddling almost twice as fast as Sonia. The bow of his kayak lurched right then left as his power strokes disoriented his craft. He extended his arms forward with a determination that literally lifted him off the seat. His paddle cut into the murky liquid, and his whole body drove the water back. Sonia was saying something delicately to him as her even, unhurried strokes propelled her craft down with the current, the bow straight and steady.

"Is Keith okay?" I asked Mike.

"I don't think he is," Mike answered. "He's acting panicky, a little erratic. Sonia is sticking with him through this stretch, just to keep an eye on him."

"That sounds good. Did Derek ask her to do it?" I asked, hoping he wouldn't hear a jealous hint in my voice.

"No, I think she just picked up on the panic back at the last stop and is trying to help," Mike said. "I don't think he's her type, don't worry."

Mike and I rounded a bend and saw the group gathering near the left bank. We arrived and Derek began.

"The Middle Fork merges just below, but there is no telling what to expect. So, I want everybody to stay put right here while I walk over that ridge and get a look at it. There is a way through it, but it won't be anything like we're used to."

Keith blurted, "How hard could it be? Let's just run it. We just need to get off this river. We have an injured person. We're wasting time!"

The group fell silent. Sonia turned her head slightly to the left and looked directly at me. Her eyes widened and rolled to the side. Derek unceremoniously dropped his head, and the only sound was the low rumble of the river.

"It won't take long. This is the right way to do it. I've been running rivers for ten years." He paused. "When the raft gets here, get a snack and fill up your water bottles. I'll be back."

He looked over the group, resting his gaze briefly on Mike, Sonia, and then me as if to gauge our states of mind. He took a deep breath, turned, and sprinted up the hill. We beached our boats high on the shore to prevent any sudden current from floating them away and began stretching our legs and aimlessly milling around. The atmosphere was heavy, and when the raft arrived it was a welcome relief to just open the granola bars and fill up the water bottles, all mindless tasks that kept us busy and made the waiting easier.

I walked over to Sonia, and we talked about paddling and the boats and the trash in the water—all small talk. She seemed distracted, and I felt that special connection between us fading away until I noticed she was keeping an eye on Keith.

"Is he all right?" I asked.

"No, really panicking. He's the biggest danger out here," she said in almost a whisper.

"The river is pretty tough," I replied. "We're in a small flood situation."

"That's why everybody needs to have their wits about them, and Keith…well, what can I say?"

I watched Sonia form the words, articulate and exact while her lips moved judiciously, her mouth opening only enough to pronounce each syllable precisely. The heat of the afternoon sun felt blistering standing on shore. Sonia pulled her T-shirt off and wrapped it around her waist. The scant bikini top covered little, and I watched a bead of sweat roll from her neck into the soft cleavage of her breasts. She caught my gaze and returned it.

"What's your life about?" she asked. "Who are the people in your life?"

"A son and a daughter and a company—pretty boring, I guess," I replied.

"I'll bet it's not all that boring," she said and then looked to her right and quickly back to me. "Where is he? Where is Keith? One of the kayaks is gone."

Mike ran to the edge of the water and waded in to his knees. He faced downstream into the glaring afternoon sun, raising his right hand to shade his eyes.

"He's headed downstream," Mike shouted.

Sonia bolted for her boat. With no effort she leaped into the seat, scooped up her two-bladed paddle, and in seconds was in the flow of the river going after Keith. I looked at Mike watching Sonia as she darted away.

"What's going on?" I practically yelled at Mike.

"Listen, let them go. We wait for Derek and the raft. That's the plan. Stick to the plan. They'll be all right. Sonia will catch up to him and talk him into waiting for us."

I stood on the bank next to Mike, staring into the sun, watching two kayaks turn into specks on the light-drenched river. What was Sonia doing? She took off after Keith like he was a blood relative. Why did she feel responsibility for him? They disagree on almost everything. She trumped him in half the shootouts they had on politics, and I thought some of it was brutal. Maybe there was a spark between those two that I had been missing, I thought, though with an uneasy disbelief.

I jumped in my kayak while shouting back at Mike that I needed to catch them. His admonition to hold up before the Middle Fork could barely be heard over the river's growling thunder. I joined the downstream flow of the river, paddling hard for about five minutes, until I could see them ahead of me.

They were in the middle of the raging flow, stalled in a large, tranquil eddy formed behind a giant boulder. As I got nearer, I saw Sonia's head jerking back and forth, front to back, her mouth moving quickly. The quiet subtleties in her speech were gone. She was yelling at Keith, who was shaking his head side to side. The roar of the current prevented me from hearing either of their voices, but then I could see what Derek had feared the most. The Middle Fork flowed into our river at a sixty-degree angle, but the calm flow had turned into a torrent. The merging river was swollen over its banks, and the raging water flooded onto the barren shoreline. Where the rivers met, a six-foot wave formed a giant wall of water curling upstream toward us. Rocks and small boulders churned and rotated through this devil's soup. I had never seen anything like it. This was no place for rubber kayaks. The vacation was over. This was true peril.

My boat rushed toward the arguing couple as I hit the fast water just above them and a high, white-capped curl threw me to the right. I leaned into the mouth of the wave, shoved my paddle deep into its throat, and pulled forward. My boat leveled out and shot through the wave. I made two hard sweep strokes on my right side to pull into the eddy with Keith and Sonia, but the current swept me past them. Landing near a small, shallow rock ledge, I got out of my boat and waded in two feet of water to the dry granite. The shouting appeared to have stopped on the river. I threw my hands straight into the air and waved them back and forth to get their attention. I motioned them over to my perch with desperate gestures of my right hand when Sonia's hand patted the top of her head, the river signal for "okay."

She turned the bow of her boat upstream and caught the flow. With three firm sweep strokes, she directed her boat in a straight trajectory to my rock beach. Keith seemed to be following Sonia, then his kayak suddenly rotated, and he was swept backward through the bottom of the eddy directly downstream. The strong current caught the stern and rotated it again, pointing him toward the opposite bank. Keith paddled ferociously. Right and left strokes, back strokes, but he could not gain control. He spun several more times, and finally the eddy spit him out into the speeding current. Hitting a small wave backward, the boat's impact almost turned it over. His paddle was jolted from his hands. His left hand lurched into the water, grabbing for the floating paddle, but it was whisked away out of his reach by the white, foaming current.

Sonia jumped out of her craft and quickly waded over to shore. We ran to a high point on our rock island and watched as Keith rode his rudderless craft down to a hapless fate. His boat rotated, hitting a series of ripples bow first. Then the boat slowly spun sideways, and Keith grabbed both gunnels of his boat as he hit the six-foot wall of water. Debris from upstream churned under the gurgling soup, and as the yellow boat was absorbed by the water, we saw a giant uprooted tree being thrown out of the caldron onto the surface and on top of Keith. Sonia let go a blood-curdling scream that echoed throughout the canyon. Then she let her face drop into the palms of her hands and started sobbing. I reached over and touched the small of her back. She turned and embraced me with both arms, laying her head on my shoulder.

I held tightly for half a minute as her near hysteria died down and her body relaxed. As her head rose from my shoulder, she pulled away from my embrace.

"Let's go," she said and took a step toward our beached kayaks.

"We can't go down there! These little boats can't run that water. Hell, no boat can run that. It would be suicide," I yelled, mostly out of panic.

"Come on," she shouted as she continued down the jagged rock surface to the boats.

I ran after her down to the water with no intention of either following Keith into that abyss or allowing Sonia to go.

"Sonia, stop right there. You cannot go down that river. I mean it," I shouted over the bellowing of the water.

"We're not going down the river. We're going across to the other side. If he's alive, maybe we can fish him out below the choppy water. I think we can walk over that ridge and down to the bank over there. We have to get to the other side," she said in a calm, authoritative voice.

"Yeah, but there's no way to cross right here. It's too fast. One mistake and we'll join Keith."

"Look at that eddy on the other side, about thirty yards down. We run the current down the middle, paddle hard right just above that boulder sticking out," she shouted. "Do you see where I mean?"

"Yeah, I see it, but—"

She didn't let my thought form into words, because she didn't want to hear them.

"Paddle hard right there," she said. "The bow should move into the eddy, and as it does, back stroke on the left and the upstream current of the eddy will pull you in. Then just paddle to the bank."

I thought Sonia had crossed over to hysteria. The best chance for success for that little plan was 50 percent. The other fifty involved certain death.

"Look! Slow down. We need to walk these boats up a few hundred yards and cross up there. We can wait for the others," I retorted.

"There's no time. He still might have a chance. We've got to get—"

This time I cut her off.

"Keith is dead. He is drowned or crushed or both. You saw that tree come down on top of him, and…that water has thousands of pounds of force. Get a grip!" I was screaming over the roar of the river.

I stood face to face with Sonia as we argued. I was adamant, and she was cocksure of herself. Neither of us wanted to give ground. It was a matter of life and death for us both. For her, it was Keith's life. For me, it was our lives. It was my turn in the argument, and I started at her, yelling in her face. Suddenly her right hand darted behind my neck. She cupped the curve of my neck and pulled my head down level with hers. She rocked forward on her toes, and when her mouth met mine, I felt the tension leave my body. She held her warm lips to mine, and I slowly surrounded her body with each of my arms, one at a time, locking them around her lower back. Our lips parted, and she looked at me for a split second before I kissed her again. My arms tightened around her, and the soft flesh of her lips melted my resolve to argue. Now we would walk upriver and wait for the others, I thought. It was still going to be a long afternoon. If we found Keith at all, it would be a terrible sight. We would have to load his body on the raft to take him back, and how was the raft going to get down through this stretch anyway?

"Okay, let's go," she said.

Sonia broke away from our embrace, jumped in her boat, and darted out to the main channel. Without thinking, I followed, paddling ferociously. She pointed her boat downstream, heading straight for the big rock. About eight feet out, she dug her paddle deep into the swirling water and executed three wide strokes on the right. On the last one, she leaned so far right, I thought the kayak would tip over, but instead the thrust of the paddle heaved the boat to the opposite side and her bow surged into the eddy. A quick back stroke on the left and she settled into the quiet water.

I paddled hard toward the rock and started my sweep strokes as instructed. My bow started to turn left, but then I felt the boat lift up from the back and undulate forward. A freak wave tossed my boat off its trajectory and head-on into the big rock. The right gunnel scraped against the smooth granite, and the force of the water pinned the craft against the rock. The roar of the Middle Fork was deafening, and the spray from the churning, gurgling water pelted my eyes. I tried to push off the rock with the blade of my paddle. I had lost sight of anything but the water and my nemesis, the rock, when I felt a small strand of line lay itself softly across my shoulder. The end had a small red-and-white buoy attached. I looked over my shoulder and saw Derek on the bank looping the other end around the only stout tree in sight. I tied the rope to the ring on the front of my kayak and started paddling for my life. Derek stood in back of the tree and pulled his end of the line. The coils of the rope slid around the tree as he backed up. As my boat broke away, I made the mistake of leaning away from the rock, into the current. The left gunnel dipped level to the water's surface, allowing a small flow of the river's rushing rage into the craft. Then, in a split second, the gunnel plunged below the waterline, under the rushing flow, and the boat filled and tilted left at the same moment. As the kayak made its half turn to upside down, I felt myself gently being laid into the cold, brown, liquid fury. The bright, glaring afternoon sun turned to black as the boat flipped on top of my bobbing head and shoulders. I let go of my paddle and grabbed a taught cord inside the boat, while my knees grazed and bounced off the submerged mass of the rock as my boat and I joined the downward flow. The standard-issue red life vest kept my head upright, but the spray and churning of the water splashed into my eyes and mouth, wiping away any feelings of safety. Fear and uncertainty piled on like a three-hundred-pound linebacker. My legs dangled in the deep current, and I managed to pull them together in a halfhearted scissors kick while pushing on the upriver side of the kayak. A sliver of light peaked through the gap as the boat tossed on the surface, but the kayak would not right itself. All outside sound was muffled, and I was stuck following Keith into certain death. What seemed like a lifetime was only a few seconds, while the river veteran, Derek, held tight to my lifeline and reeled me toward the shore into the safety of a swirling eddy. When my feet touched the river bottom, I stood, extended both arms straight up, and tossed the boat over my head to the side.

Standing there like a cold, wet rat, I shouted at Derek on the shore, "Did you see Keith?"

"Yeah, I saw Keith, but I also saw you," he replied. "What kind of trick was that? You have a death wish?"

"Christ!" I said almost under my breath. "It's a long story."

A few minutes passed by in silence as Derek pulled the kayak to land and I waded to the shoreline and sat down. Fear and confusion took over my body, and I stared at the river but only saw white space in front of my eyes. My mind went blank.

"I saw Keith go in, didn't see him come out," he said. "It's pretty bad. Walk up to the others and tell them to bring the raft down here and wait for me. I'm going downstream to look for him."

"I'm going with you," Sonia said as she appeared from around a giant boulder.

Derek paused, looking at Sonia and back at me.

After a long few seconds he said, "Okay, let's all go."

14

J ust a few days before, when the twin-engine Air Idaho plane dropped into the town of Salmon, I couldn't have foreseen the turmoil ahead. From the air the sporadic snow blanket on the rugged mountains looked like a patchwork of white and brown. The raw rock peaks were windswept and, from five thousand feet, breathtaking. My mind digressed to a similarly spectacular view of the Rocky Mountains from a Boeing 747 at thirty thousand feet. The view from there is like watching a nature video in the comfort of your own den. But from a fraction of that altitude, those white, craggy peaks in Idaho were more real, and from beneath their spotty, white blanket called out a warning. I was warned, now I knew.

We were in a disaster situation, and Keith could be dead. Survival was the only mandate. My mind wandered, and I had trouble staying focused on where we were and what we were doing. I guess I wasn't sure what we had to do or who was doing it or what would happen next. I was in shock, or something like it. My mind flashed second by second on a thousand things, it seemed. Then the last few days on the river stuck in my thoughts, white water, fishing, business, kids, and Muffin. I thought about how irritating the political discussions had been for me. I was being tolerant, but I didn't like it all that much. I was used to controlling my surroundings; that's what you have to do, running a business. But no one could control this river and this flood, even though Derek was trying. Maybe they would have all mellowed out if this flooding hadn't happened, I thought. All those political arguments had no meaning to us now. Sonia confronted Keith so vehemently, and now she was beside herself over his plight. Politics becomes so personal and vicious, and people lose track of the topics and the problems and, most of all, the solutions. They don't agree on the solutions. Or worse, they don't even agree on the problems.

I was walking behind Derek and Sonia, struggling to keep up. Their eyes were straight ahead, fixed on their task. I felt like sitting down, slightly dizzy. The afternoon sun beat down, beads of sweat rolled down my chest, and my thoughts kept rambling.

The world seemed to go into slow motion. The sounds of the river dulled and then vanished altogether. The light flashes gave way to a flat glow. My mind raced on, frantic to think this thing through and solve it—right now. I didn't have the wherewithal to wonder why.

I raised my leg to mount a large rock, and my right knee gave way under my own weight, almost throwing me to the ground. The sun flashed in my eyes, and I felt the dizzy world all around me.

Sonia glanced back over her shoulder as she stepped to the top of a small granite formation. She suddenly stopped and turned to face me.

"You're white as a sheet. Sit down right now," she demanded.

Derek stopped and turned but did not say a word. They both walked back to me and sat down.

"I can't seem to focus, and I'm feeling a little faint," I admitted.

Derek handed me a bottle of water but nobody spoke. The emotional exhaustion had caught up with all of us, and the weight of our predicament was just now sinking in fully. Sonia wedged herself in between two rocks and rested her back on a third while Derek sat stoically, back straight, his gaze straight ahead. My eyes closed, and I dozed off for a few minutes while sitting straight up. I had no dreams or thoughts of politics or kids or any of the rest of it. Just a blank mind, thank god.

I woke up to Derek's gentle voice, "Jonathan, how are you feeling? We need to cover some ground. If we are going to find him, we need to do it now."

My eyes opened slowly, but right away I could tell the nap worked miracles. I felt more focused and the dizziness had passed.

15

We followed Derek over a steep rock mound, across a gray granite ledge, and down to the riverbank. I scanned the area for any sign of Keith or his kayak but saw nothing. Sonia waded to a giant boulder just offshore, climbed to the top, and surveyed the swollen riverbanks downstream. Nothing.

"What are we going to do?" Sonia asked.

"I'm not leaving anybody down here, and that's final," Derek said, with a solid resolve back in his voice. "We'll find him. You guys walk upstream and look on both sides. I'm going down around that bend. Here, blow this whistle if you find something."

He handed me a silver whistle tied onto a loop of old cotton string, then turned and trotted downriver through the trees. I opened my hand and looked at the whistle. A bolt of sunshine reflected from the chrome surface, causing my eyes to squint for a quick second. I raised it to my lips and took a breath, ready to exhale and force a high-pitched blast out the other end. Sonia had taken a few steps along the bank and was looking upstream scanning for clues to Keith's whereabouts. I looked down and unceremoniously closed my hand around the whistle again, slipping it into my front pocket without making a sound. She and I walked for a few minutes and then she stopped, turned toward me, and took my hand. Her rosy cheeks had turned pale, and she looked like a changed person. Her confident resolve was replaced by uncertainty and fear.

"Look, things are tense and there's a lot of anxiety out here and sometimes people do things they wouldn't normally do. I understand that, and I want you to know that if you want to forget our little smooch up there, it's okay with me. I'll understand."

"You really meant it then?" I asked.

"Well, yeah. I don't go around kissing random boys, at least not too often."

"I'm not exactly a boy anymore."

I pulled her closer and kissed her. She put her arms around my back and her body pressed against mine. We took a breath and kissed again. Whatever this turned out to be in the long run was irrelevant right now. I liked this intimacy with Sonia, but we were both shaky and needed assurance. I thought it was all probably temporary, wouldn't last. Just deal with the panic and fear now, I thought, and keep it light.

"You know, I'm kind of a square and I have grown kids and I don't live in L.A. Is this a one-river stand for you?" I joked, hoping she would go along with that mood change.

"We can make it what we want. I know what I want."

We stood locked in an embrace, and I kissed her again. Her soft lips parted slightly, and the faint hint of her warm breath sent a shiver down to my toes.

Sonia and I fanned out along the riverbank, which was thick with debris caught in bushes and small trees that normally were high above the waterline that time of year. I hoped the red paddle jacket would give away Keith's location, but couldn't be sure it would still be on him. Pulling up logs and limbs, I looked in pools and under bushes, but found no trace. Finally, I stopped while balancing on two rounded boulders, the soles of my treaded river shoes clinging to the polished granite. I looked upstream in frustration. That's when I saw the red fabric shredded in narrow, uneven, long strips clinging to a brush-covered limb. I made my way along the steep bank, dipping into the water when the land receded into a sharp vertical wall, eliminating my walking path. About thirty yards up, I found Keith's jacket, or what was left of it. I looked up, my eyes scanning for any possible new clues, but saw nothing that would lead me to our lost colleague. Five wild geese descended in formation, swooping into the canyon. They hovered, gliding in midair, and then dove together just a few feet from the water's surface, wings fixed, into the headwind of a downstream air current. I stood fixated on their flight, watching the small flock round the bend in the canyon. My eyes left the birds and followed a line of sight into the heavily wooded slope beyond the river. The branches of the fur trees lining the bank formed V-shaped patterns up to the top of the ridge. Then my eye caught the birds banking right, tightly in formation, as if directed by a grand conductor. They flapped their wings in unison, still hovering what looked to be only inches from the surface, and disappeared from sight.

Just then I heard the muffled shriek of a police whistle and darted toward the sound. When I caught up with Sonia, we painstakingly worked our way down a stretch of shoreline, following the whistle, until we found Derek, who was leaning over a clump of bushes engulfed by a newly formed pool of brown water. He had broken and bent the thin twigs and was standing knee-deep in the pool. Keith's body was lying on one side wedged among a random tangle of small branches, his legs twisted and bending just below the waist in a contorted, unnatural way. A ripped, tattered shirt clung to his body, but gaping holes in it revealed his pale, sallow skin.

"He's still breathing but looks pretty broken up. It's going to take all three of us to get him to dry land. Sonia, pick up his legs just under his knees," Derek directed. "I'll support his back. Okay, lift."

Keith made no sound or movement. We laid him in the leaves on his back. His right shoulder was cinched up near his ear, and it looked like the collar bone was broken. A knee was turned sideways and twisted, and his lower leg dangled at an odd angle, but no major bleeding, at least on the surface. He was breathing evenly.

"Keith, can you hear me?" Sonia blurted, but he made no sound. "Keith?" she pleaded.

"I've got to get the raft down here. The splints and medical gear are mandatory now, and the satellite phone is there. The helicopter can pick him up about a half mile down at a burn-out from the fire in ninety-one. I'm not letting anybody die on my trip," Derek said, out of breath.

"How does the raft make it through the river from up there?" Sonia demanded.

"I have a few tricks up my sleeve. I'll bring it down. I told you, everybody gets out while I'm in charge."

Derek took off in a sprint. Like a wild young buck, he darted through the trees, around the rocks, and disappeared.

Sonia hovered over Keith, propping his head up and clearing the brush from around him. Then she sat down beside me and pulled her knees up to her chest. I laid my arm around her waist. She dropped her head on my shoulder and began to sob. I tightened my hold, and she inched closer.

"Things turned bad so quick," Sonia confided. "We went from a vacation to disaster in a matter of hours. Keith is a nice person. I can't imagine him in this situation."

"I feel the same way. But I have to say, you were chewing him up at the campfire the other night."

"Yeah, it's good-natured debate. I get a little worked up sometimes, but I thought he handled himself okay. But, really, I can't even think about it now. I just don't know about anything."

She exhaled with those words, as if using all the breath left her lungs and, with it, all her energy and resolve. There was a long silence and then she said, "Anyway, I don't take it personally. It's ideas, not people. Keith is a person and part of our group. He needs us now."

The only sound was the roar of the river for a long time while we caught our breath and thought about the dire situation we had to make sense of. I wanted to say something, anything, but nothing found its way through my lips. Keith was our biggest worry, but if he and Simon could get busted up, so could any of us. The finality of being on our own without help was a dire thought. Sonia was reaching a stress point. I knew I had to buck up and stay steady—nerves of steel—that's what was required. When Karen died, I felt like everything was caving in around me. I had been working ten-hour days to make the business successful. I had to—well, at least I thought I did—and the kids were way too young for that kind of trauma, losing their mother. I pulled myself together and got them through it and back on track. Standing tall in the hurricane—that was me, no problem. Well, the hens came home to roost, and a year later, the trauma of it all crept in. I would go to bed exhausted only to wake up in an hour buzzing like a bee. I'd break out in a cold sweat at work, shaking like a leaf. It was like battle trauma, my doctor said—post-traumatic stress. Over the years I recovered from that, but right now it was a battle again. I needed a strong game face. I didn't know how I could help, but I needed to be ready and resolved. I had trained myself to lead in business. This was a different setting and Derek was in charge, but I wanted to be ready to be a strong player.

Time was ticking by, and none of the crew showed up. Again I felt the need to say something, to get some conversation going, to get our minds off the waiting. I wanted to think of a way to lighten things up.

"So, okay, just between you and me," I finally said, "who are you, Miss Sonia? I mean, where did you come from, just what makes you tick like a precision Swiss watch, anyway?"

"Tick-tock around the clock," she answered, deflecting my probing question.

"Come on, help me out here, tell me about Sonia," I said gently.

The Swiss watch was beginning to miss a few beats, but I didn't bring that up. She didn't say a word, and the air between us thickened and crusted like a bowl of old pea soup. I was pushing, and she was in no mood to chitchat. After a long minute of silence, she spoke.

"I want to tell you a children's story that my father used to tell me. I always thought he made it up because it's a little perverse, but I kind of like it anyway."

"Okay," I said with trepidation and some measure of anticipation.

"It goes like this: Montrose de la Mouse was the oldest descendent of the original clan founders. The clan dominated the East Kingdom for over twenty generations. The kingdom was comprised of a half-acre corner in a fallow cow pasture on a hillside in the south of France, a few miles north of Nice near the French Riviera. The clan was started by two brothers, Chateau and Boudreaux, who, out to seek their fortunes, came upon a thick, grassy field next to a small thicket of wild strawberries. They stopped for an afternoon meal, and after having eaten all they could eat and stuffing their pockets with all that they could carry, walked ahead only to find a patch of lillykiles, the grass with the tasty roots that melt in your mouth just like mother's special jackydill fudge. They ate another meal, and by the time their stomachs stopped aching, they realized that there could be no better place to live than right there.

"The clan started small but grew rapidly along with the underground tunnels and subterranean chateaus for all the clan members. The thick grass in the field gave perfect cover from hawks and catywapuses that might try to sneak around and scoop up a poor, unsuspecting mouse. All the mice worked hard to build storage chambers for strawberries, roots, and seeds for the winter, but nobody worked harder than Chateau and Boudreaux. On the weekends when all the people of the clan were having picnics, three-legged races, and drinking lillykile beer, Chateau would toil alone in his laboratory working on new inventions that would bring a better life for the clan. For example, even though the underground strawberry chambers were stuffed full of the red, delicious fruit each fall, by mid-spring the produce was spoiled and covered in mildew. Chateau finally discovered, through much trial and error, that elmwood oak leaves could be coated with a thick layer of boneybak sap to virtually eliminate the moisture from the wet winter soil. Boudreaux found a way to bend one end of a boneybak thorn to form a hooked end that snuggly fastened the leaves to the dirt walls.

"The clan then realized that by the time the summer strawberries were ripe, the stored fruit from last season was still juicy and tasty. So, the next season they began selling stored berries to neighboring clans who were glad to have the winter nourishment. The next few generations of the de la Mouse clan expanded the tunnels and storage capacity so everyone had plenty to eat. Trade and commerce provided enough seeds, roots, juices, and lillykile beer for everyone. After a while the clan leaders were so busy keeping the accounts and inventories in good order that they stopped doing any of the productive work like picking the produce or cleaning tunnels. In fact, they had the workers dig deeper and wider burrows for the governing sect of the clan to house the papers and records. They added lounges and sleeping quarters and even racket courts for much-needed recreation, for many of the rulers rarely left the tunnels anymore. Workers were instructed to bring the ripest strawberries, the tastiest seeds, and the best beer to the government offices. Soon so much of the summer crop was stored and traded away to neighbors that the regular members of the clan had to forage often for extra seeds and berries to survive the winter.

"One day the governors summoned fresh-picked fruit and hot lillykile-root soup for a special celebration. They waited and waited but nobody came with the banquet meal. Finally, Montrose de la Mouse sent his nephew to check on the food, and to everyone's surprise, the tunnels and caverns were empty. Everyone had left and the governors were alone. Montrose, himself, toured the storage chambers and with shock and surprise discovered that each one was totally empty. The governors then proceeded in a group through the tunnels until they emerged into the light of an autumn day. An early-winter chill was in the air, the sky was covered with broken clouds, and the strawberry vines were stripped naked of their juicy fruit. The governors filed one by one back into the tunnel and assembled around their large oval table. All was quiet while Montrose tried to conjure up a solution befitting his great ancestors, Chateau and Boudreaux, for the winter was setting in and there was no food to be had. Alas, nothing came to mind, and he wished he had a nice, fresh glass of lillykile beer."

My eyelids felt like a ton of lead, and as soon as Sonia's story ended, I nodded off to sleep.

16

I opened my eyes and stared at the curling caps of the white waves breaking over into a brown, murky, bloated river. The red, orange, and purple reflecting from the surface of the crystal-clear water of two days ago had changed to a brown, almost olive color in the low, bright afternoon sun. The silt-filled soup carried the runoff from hundreds of miles upstream on down to the Snake and Colorado rivers and to the Gulf of Mexico. Sonia was lying still next to me. I started to turn.

"Shh! Don't move," she whispered. "Snake near Keith's head."

My eyes darted toward Keith. About two feet from his left ear, a fat, slinking reptile slithered its way slowly toward the water. We lay still behind its line of sight. The snake stopped, as if sniffing Keith, moved down next to his shoulders, and unhurriedly began to form a coil. Then I felt Sonia dart up. She grabbed a two-inch thick branch stripped of its bark by the river, and before I could blink, she slammed it into the middle of the coiling intruder. The snake turned to face Sonia, who still held the pole, and without hesitation extended its body in a massive strike at Sonia. Her right foot, which had stepped forward for her attack, was in full retreat, and the snake landed on the mushy ground just short of its target.

I rolled slowly to my side and quickly crouched on my knees. Sonia was between me and the attacking reptile. I had no idea what I was going to do and categorically had no clue what Sonia thought she was doing. As I rose, a bright burst of light flashed by my eyes. I stopped and looked at the muddy riverbank about five yards away. A small piece of aluminum stuck out of the soggy soil. In one motion, I jumped to my feet and grabbed the exposed shaft with both hands. A worn aluminum paddle blade followed the broken handle out of the mud.

Sonia arrested her withdrawal, stood firmly, and waved the stick at the snake, again challenging it. It snapped its long body into a rounded coil, waved its head in Keith's direction and then back to Sonia. Sonia gestured and jeered with the pole, and when she leaned forward with a lunge, the snake again uncoiled and struck. Its ear-piercing rattle lay still on the ground, giving it a solid base to strike from. She let out a loud scream and dropped the pole while the snake again slapped onto the ground, its full length extending like a taut rope.

When the aluminum paddle blade severed the reptile's head, its long, cylindrical body curled and undulated violently. Sonia stepped back as I ran to her and grabbed her left forearm, holding it up to look for the wound.

"Missed me. Hit the stick instead," she whispered

"But you yelled. I thought you were hit."

"I thought I was, too. It scared the hell out of me. Where did you find that paddle?"

"I saw it buried in the mud, just grabbed it and came up behind him. Glad it worked," I said.

"You're my hero. I'm yours for life."

I knew she was teasing, but when she said it, I felt a twinge in my chest. The subtle humor was a tension release for us both.

Any daydreams of our cosmic future together and living happily ever after like in the sitcoms or the endless stream of sappy movies, were shoved aside. There was no time for sentimental endings, I thought. But, the truth was there was nothing but time and waiting. We were waiting for Derek and the crew to get down here with the raft and waiting for Keith to get hauled out of here and waiting for night to fall, waiting for some food to be cooked, waiting to get off this river, waiting for Keith to die, maybe, and waiting for Sonia's warm lips on mine again. All this flashed through my mind in a split second. Then my eyes focused again on Sonia.

"Was that bastard going after Keith?" I asked.

"Hell, I don't know what snakes do, I'm a business major."

I scooped up the severed head with the paddle and hurled it into the current. Sonia started clearing more brush from around Keith, who didn't move.

"Do you think Derek will make it down soon?" she asked.

"He may have to empty the raft to float it past the Middle Fork. Maybe the others have to walk over the ridge, I don't know."

"Can Simon make it?" she asked.

"Well, no broken bones, going slow, they'll get him over. He has to make it, though. Nobody can float that stretch in a rubber kayak."

17

The air was dead calm, and the bloated river flowed past us with a low rumble. A large, round fire pit held a roaring blaze. The heat furled straight up, causing a continuous sharp quiver in the branches just above the pit. Derek's crew had emptied the supply raft for its run past the Middle Fork juncture. Then they loaded it back up and floated it down to camp. While Mike and I cooked the chili, Sonia helped make Keith comfortable. He regained consciousness just before dark and suffered through an awkward process of fitting splints on his shoulder and knee. An ace bandage held them all together, but the slightest movement caused a sharp pain from his shoulder straight down his spine. He became slightly more moveable as the Vicodin and codeine took effect, but I knew tomorrow was going to be tough for him. Still, the mood around camp softened and people's spirits lightened up. There was a bit of joking, and I even saw Sonia's run-and-skip move around the camp.

Walking over to Keith's tent, I could hear Derek talking in a low, measured voice. Although I wanted to ask Keith why he took off like that, Derek was focusing on getting him down the river. Where was the pain? What could he move? How did he feel? Derek was standing tall in the hurricane. He was in charge, and I knew that we were going to do things his way, till we got home, and I was glad about that.

Derek had gotten through to the ranger station on the satellite phone, and a helicopter was meeting us in the morning, but we had to float Keith a half mile down the river, which showed no signs of calming down. He was complaining about pain in his stomach and lower back, and we feared he had internal damage. This was the deepest part of this ancient gorge, where roads did not exist. From rim to river was a mile deep and rim to rim was at least ten miles across. Rescue teams floating down were ruled out because of the flooding. We were on our own.

Mike and I set up several tents, putting Simon's gear in one of them. Simon was recovering but still dizzy and needed help getting settled for the night. Back in civilization he would have been in a hospital being treated for a concussion. He hobbled over the ridge earlier with the help of two guides and now sat with us around the fire silent and dazed as Sonia and Derek rejoined us and sat down.

"That booger almost got me at the top of the run," Derek said. "After that big hole on the left, the current goes directly toward the big wall of water. I had to fight like hell to keep out of it."

"It looked six or seven feet high from where we stood. What do you think?" Sonia asked.

"That seems about right. The raft would have been chewed up like a dishrag, and I'd be sharing the splints with Keith. Three-foot-diameter boulders are churning around in that mess. I can't believe Keith is still breathing."

"How can water lift a rock weighing hundreds of pounds? Okay, it could roll them along the bottom, but lift them to the top?" I asked.

"It doesn't seem rational, I admit, but it's really a simple thing," Derek answered. "The fast water picks up sand and silt, which is suspended, and the sheer mass of that concoction is heavier than the big rocks. All of the deep canyons were carved out by these flash floods hurling rocks into the side walls. That was all before we started controlling the flooding. Actually, it was before humans walked the planet."

"But still, that's a lot of carving for a few rocks," I said.

"A few million years and it gets the job done. Things take time," Derek said.

"Did you get a look at that snake?" I asked.

"Rattler. Poisonous. Good thing you killed it," Derek said softly.

"Well, I thought Sonia was going to teach it the polka. I mean, she was fearless with that monster," I said.

Derek looked over at Sonia and said, "You're a city girl with a lot of guts, that's for sure."

We sat around the fire finishing the hot chili; the arrogant boasting, arguments about politics, and sharp-witted frivolity of previous nights was absent. Mike sipped a beer, and a bottle of Jack Daniels, from some unknown source, slowly passed around the group. The three bright stars of Orion's belt stared at me once again, but this time through a clear, blue sky. I had no inspiring insights, and I gazed up with thoughts only of tomorrow and getting off this river. The group thinned out, and Mike and I sat alone in silence around the smoldering blaze for a while. Time for sleep, I thought. I got up without a word and headed back to my tent.

When I got there, the front door flaps were flung to the sides so I stooped forward, ducked my head, and started to shimmy into the small, narrow enclosure. A flashlight suddenly illuminated my feet, and I looked up, a little startled, at the light's source.

"Don't get the wrong idea. I'm just in here for snake protection. You killed the first one. I'm counting on you for defense."

I stood kneeling, frozen for a few seconds. Neither one of us said a word. Then I lifted my right hand and reached forward. I cupped Sonia's soft cheek in my palm and then gently kissed her mouth. Her lips were soft and wet, melting like warm honey against mine. Her arms opened and pulled me into the tent next to her. She lifted her head and kissed me, then rolled onto her back, dragging me on top, while her hand rested on the small of my back and pressed my body against hers. The small flashlight slipped under the sleeping bag, and the tent was dark except for a glimmer of moonlight seeping through the thin nylon walls.

18

A *young boy stood at home plate staring intently at an infield in the center of a sun-roasted baseball diamond in Murfreesboro, Tennessee. As the pitcher's foot pawed the mound and he contemplated the next pitch, the slow pace of the game was unnerving the young batter. His feet would not stand still, his eyes darted, and his whole body vibrated with the expectation of the next pitch. He was capable of swinging the bat and making solid connection with the ball, but patience to wait, to lurk in the batter's box looking for the opportunity of a hittable ball down the middle of the plate, eluded the young player. The first pitch came flying across the plate, and the boy twisted his waist and shoulders forward. Arms and bat followed with a ferocious cut through the thick, humid, Southern air. High and outside, should have let it go, wait for a better one, take a breath, step out of the batter's box, make the pitcher wait, control the pace of the game. I knew what to do, but I couldn't tell him. I wanted him to look at me, but he kept staring at the pitcher and the infield. Suddenly he stepped out of the box and looked at the left-field bleachers and gave a quick wave with his right hand. Fourth-row center, waving back, was a forty-ish, slim man with a slightly receding hairline dressed in business slacks and a short-sleeve white shirt. He wore aviator sunglasses but no hat. It was his dad, I was sure. I tried to get a better look but couldn't see. The man looked familiar to me.*

"I was hitting well in practice this week. Coach says I need to settle in," the boy said, as if talking directly to the fourth-row bleachers.

"Just wait for a good one and watch the ball leave the pitcher's hand. Keep your eye on that ball. You'll hit it," his dad said in a quiet, confident voice from the distant bleachers.

I glanced back at home plate, and the boy was still looking deep in the outfield. Then he stroked the dirt with his left foot and glared down the third-base line. The next pitch found the center of his white hickory bat. The third baseman extended his glove and leaped into the air, but the ball soared into left field, farther and farther, until it disappeared in a murky haze.

My eyes opened slowly, and I focused on the top of the moon-drenched tent only two feet above. I felt like rubbing my eyes but didn't want to expend the effort to pull my arms out of the warm bag. Sonia was beside me facing the tent wall. She had a small stocking cap on her head covering the only part of her body that was not deep in the sleeping bag. I bent sideways and looked out of the open tent door. The fire was smoldering, the air was calm, and the camp was totally quiet. After zipping up the tent flap, I buried myself back in the bag next to Sonia and fell asleep again.

19

The early-morning light faintly filled the tent as I began to focus, opening one sleepy eye at a time.

"Hey there, snake killer," Sonia whispered in my ear.

I turned to see her brown eyes wide open and staring at me. She didn't wear makeup and didn't need it. The glow from her rosy cheeks was back, and the gleam in her eyes gave her a natural beauty. She had an inner attractiveness that transcended the physical, a deeply confident character. But, even the toughest people can go over the cliff, and Sonia definitely edged past her limits yesterday. Today she sounded like her old self. Everybody's vulnerable sometime, I thought.

Anyway, this romance thing was going a little fast for even me. A fearless titan of business, here I was helpless in the clutches of love.

"You're quite a chick," I said softly.

"Just what I needed early in the morning, a derogatory term that equates me to a small, defenseless animal," she replied.

I made no reply and waited to see how much trouble I was in. She shoved the palm of her hand against my shoulder and rolled me over on my back. Before I could resist, she crawled over and slammed her lips on mine in a hard, fierce kiss. Both of her hands darted to the sides of my rib cage, and she began tickling. I rolled from side to side, trying to break her grip. She kept her mouth plastered to mine, muffling my giddy laughter. Finally, I broke loose.

"Okay, okay, you're not a chick," I blurted.

"I like being a chick. It means you have to do everything for me. I'm helpless and need waiting on. Let's get started. Peel me a grape."

"You're not a chick. I give up," I pleaded.

"This must mean you're a 'cool dude,'" she said. "Let's see, what do you need to be the coolest? A mustang convertible, or maybe a yellow and black Mini Cooper—drop-top, of course. A spike haircut—yeah, get rid of that frumpy look. You need some of those pants that hang around your hips to make sure your boxer shorts can be seen by the general public. I've got it, for more formal occasions you need those four-hundred-dollar blue jeans that are ripped up and shredded. I'm giving you a real makeover, mister."

She wore a huge grin and was reveling like a little girl in this fantasy. I rose up on my elbow and stopped her banter with a gentle kiss as my left hand caressed the tickle-center of her rib cage tenderly.

She pulled away and whispered, "Don't you dare."

Without a word, my hand rotated inward to stroke her bare breast.

"That's better," she said.

20

The rocks were covered with a light layer of morning dew, and even the usually dry summer moss had a soft, rain-soaked look. The guides moved like a precision machine packing the raft. A five-foot slab of plywood that had been the platform for strapping sleeping bags and kitchen gear was tied securely across the back of the raft. A tree had been selected about fifty yards from the riverbank, and the large food coolers, tents, and other gear were being piled next to it.

"Bag your tent and sleeping gear, Casanova, and put it next to the tree," Derek shouted while looking straight at me. "A boat will float down next week to pick it all up."

"Okay. What can I help with?" I asked.

"Put some padding on that slab of plywood. We're going to strap Keith down to get through Gunbarrel rapid. The helicopter pickup is just beyond it at Horsecreek Camp. The Forest Service cleared a helipad after the big fire. The rapid is a class two, but it'll run fast today."

"How is he?" I asked.

"The shoulder is about the same, the knee is turning black, and his stomach is swelling. There's coffee and some bread and jelly. That's it for breakfast," Derek explained, breaking away with a brisk walk toward the boats.

Sonia was crouched next to Keith when I stuck my head into his tent.

"You holding in there, buddy?" I asked, knowing the answer was not a good one.

"I'll be whipping Sonia around the dance floor tonight, no problem," Keith said with a quiet whisper.

"Yeah you will. We're putting you in first class for the remainder of the flight, buddy. Hold your own," I said in my best good-ole-boy banter.

I backed slowly out of the small entrance and stood quietly alone next to the tent under a century-old white pine tree. I looked up to see stripped lower branches, remnants of old limbs broken at the ends still holding on to the massive trunk, still part of the proud tree but weary and useless. No breeze rustled through the evergreen canopy. The dead air was only a blank canvass for the drone of the river, always there. I could hear the muffled voices of Sonia and Keith, and then, as if on stage delivering a lecture, Keith started talking in a clear, distinct voice.

"You need to know about the book," he began.

"Just take it easy, now," Sonia broke in. "You can tell me all about it when you're stronger."

"No, listen, I want you to hear this," he insisted. "I didn't ever want to write a book for a group of tree huggers. Most of what's in there is questionable science made up by...well, I don't know who wrote that stuff."

"Wait," Sonia said. "You mean, you didn't write it?"

"No. I didn't know much about global warming at the time. The publisher called me from New York and asked if I would be a part of this book they were putting together that coincided with my research about global temperature variations. They would provide most of the material through a ghostwriter, but they wanted me to write a chapter on species' reaction to climate change. I had no work on that, but they offered a five-thousand-dollar advance for the entire piece, so I dummied up a chapter on it, thinking they would add it to the research work that they wanted to publish."

"Dummied it up?" Sonia replied.

"I had heard a little about it, so I wrote up what I knew, like I was an expert. No big deal, I did it a thousand times in college. Everybody does."

"Keith, I can't believe you are telling me this," Sonia said. "That book was massive, and it made you millions of dollars."

"Exactly," he continued in almost a whisper. "When the book came out, I was in shock. It was a best seller immediately. I got calls for interviews and TV appearances, but I didn't know anything about the book that actually came out, or this whole subject of warming. So, I rooted around and found a lawyer—I'd never needed a lawyer before—to stop that book from being distributed with my name on it. He got nowhere for a couple of months, and then a six-hundred-thousand-dollar check arrived. It was an advance royalty payment. I'd never seen that much money before. Anyway, the ball was rolling, and I couldn't stop it."

"This is blowing my mind," Sonia said after a brief silence. "I didn't think things like that happened. That book was fake? Is that what I'm hearing?"

"It was real, all right. It's just I didn't write it, and I couldn't verify the science of this whole global warming theory. There is a fine line between dealing with facts and making a point. What I mean is that if all these facts, which are inconclusive, are interpreted one way, it's not seen as urgent, and nobody cares. If they are looked at a different way, the argument takes on a more compelling tone."

"You mean the science behind this isn't real?"

"It's genuine data, but the interpretation of it is skewed so the man-made global warming argument would be compelling."

"What about all this carbon emission rhetoric?" Sonia asked.

"It looks like carbon dioxide is increasing in the atmosphere, but the man-made portion may be only around one percent of the increase. Nobody really knows where it's coming from. But the rub here is that carbon dioxide is a poor greenhouse gas. Water vapor accounts for ninety-eight percent of the greenhouse effect. Carbon dioxide is not much of a factor, at least not much that anybody can prove."

There was a pause from Keith, and it seemed Sonia couldn't muster a reply. Then in a low voice Keith continued.

"Carbon is less than four-tenths of a percent of the atmosphere. It's fairly inconsequential. Anyway, weather changes all the time in areas, including the polar regions, but the primary determinant to actual global climate change is the orbital variations of the earth and sun."

"I'm not sure I follow you," Sonia said.

"Our existence on this planet is dependent on the sun. Without it, this would be a frozen ball of rock. The earth rotates on an angle, and that angle changes a few degrees over long periods of time, putting some areas closer and some further away from the light source." Keith stopped and took a long breath. "That's the primary source of climate change."

"Where are all the carbon dioxide increases coming from?" Sonia asked.

"There are a lot of possible sources," Keith continued. "Undersea volcanic eruptions can produce huge amounts of carbon dioxide that no scientist can measure. The huge population increases over the last two hundred years could be an additional source. Every person exhales carbon dioxide when they breathe. No scientist has a complete picture."

"So what did you do about the book?" Sonia asked.

"What could I do? I practically memorized the whole book, did the interviews, and went on TV. My career skyrocketed, and I made a ton of money."

There was a long pause; the wind still lay calm, and only the river spoke its whining reply. Keith was talking through the codeine, babbling on, I thought. Nobody was saying it, but we all knew that he might not make it. Was this his last confession? No, it's just the codeine, I thought.

"Whether the science is right or not, there is a huge benefit to this entire campaign," Keith spoke, breaking the quiet, his raspy, strained voice trailing off after each sentence. "And this is what I feel good about. We are able to hold polluters accountable and clean up the environment. There is a momentum toward sustainable energy, today, that would never have happened without our movement."

"Sustainable is good, Keith," Sonia said in a slightly patronizing way.

But, lying? I thought to myself.

"If the global warming theory is right, we could see huge changes that will affect agriculture, snow, and rainfall. Whole populations could be wiped out. But, the feedback loops could work in our favor and dissipate this pollution faster than we think. The truth is, nobody really knows." He paused and there was silence. "The pollution cleanup has got to be done, and everybody needs to help, Sonia."

Derek's voice echoed through the campsite. He was giving instructions, and we needed to get moving.

Sonia opened the flap and emerged from the tent looking up at me, startled. She didn't expect to see me, but her expression acknowledged that I had heard the whole thing.

"Wow," I said under my breath.

Sonia nestled her cheek onto my chest and laid her head on my shoulder.

"How far to the pickup?" she asked with a sad resolve in her voice.

"About half a mile to the camp and another mile to the vans, one rapid."

"He can't take much jostling. He's bad, really bad," she replied. "I guess it was his confession. He's a sweet guy."

We both felt like talking about this astonishing revelation, just as a way of trying to understand what it meant to us and, Christ, the whole world, but there was no time, and this was not the place.

21

When I got to the riverbank, Mike was in his kayak executing turns in a patch of still water. He looked up and nodded but said nothing. Mike was dealing with the stress in his own way. Simon stood silently on the bank facing downriver. He turned toward me; his right arm rose slowly till his hand touched the bill of his Los Angeles Dodgers hat in a "good morning" gesture.

"You kayaking today?" I asked, not thinking it was a good idea this soon after his injury.

"I'm feeling better today. No dizziness. The swelling is down. They have their hands full with Keith. I can handle it," Simon declared with a firm resolve.

"After we meet the helicopter, we have about a mile stretch before the takeout," I said, trying to sound positive.

"I've been through tougher stuff than this."

He paused, settled back on his heels, and then took a long, deep breath.

"When I was a kid I lived in Iran. The Shah was running things then. There was some favoritism, and the rich got richer, but there was order. And more important, you could get an education and a career was there if you worked hard."

He paused again and seemed to be waiting for the words to formulate in his mind.

"Then the religious fanatics moved in. That was when the American embassy was stormed and taken over. You probably remember that. The whole thing took place in about four square blocks in Tehran." Simon ambled around the small beach as he talked.

"Watching it on TV, it looked like the whole country was coming apart," I said softly.

"That's television for you. They fill a twenty-seven-inch screen with four blocks of chaos. But anyway, the country started to change radically after that. The clerics took over the government, and policies and religion restricted freedom of speech, trade, and education. The bottom dropped out of the economy, and if it weren't for oil revenue, things would have been really bad. Never planned to go back, but I made a few unplanned trips."

"What did you do when you went back?" I asked.

Simon paused, shuffled his feet in an uncomfortable little dance, and said, "Let's just say I had to take care of some family business."

My mind churned with a plethora of questions, but my mouth did not move, and no words were spoken for several quiet minutes. What was this deep, dark secret that Simon was hiding? What kind of surreptitious past did this good-natured physician have? Finally he turned halfway toward me in an accommodating gesture and spoke in a low, gentle voice like you would when you have grown a certain amount of trust in a person. I felt like some truths were going to be revealed, and my curiosity was going to be quenched.

"The best moment of my life was a dance I had in Seattle in 1979," he said. "A waltz. I was at a ballroom dancing class—a little shy and a little lonely."

"What do they say, 'I don't mind being lonesome, I just don't want to be lonely'?" I interjected.

"Precisely," he said. "Anyway, for some reason they were playing a very schmaltzy version of 'The Tennessee Waltz.' It was an old ballroom—worn-out paint, creaky floors, those wooden chairs with padded, blue cushions with about half of them loosing their stuffing. A bright green spotlight was mounted on the wall shining on a rotating glass ball that reflected tiny specks of light everywhere. I had been eyeing this very beautiful girl and finally got up the courage to walk across the room to ask her to dance. When she looked up, her green eyes seemed to open like windows to a new world. Her light brown hair broke on top of her shoulders, and her cream complexion even glowed in that dark room. But what made it the best was the way she glided in my arms across the floor, making every step effortless. She was a much better dancer than me but made me feel like Fred Astaire. We danced the whole song, and on the last note I pulled my hand up from her waist to the middle of her back, shifted my weight to my left foot, and dipped her backward. She took my cue like a ballerina, arched her back, and dropped her head below her shoulders, making a gentle curve from the tip of her toe to the top of her head."

I stood speechless. I was getting the secret all right. Whatever clandestine adventure I wanted to pry out of Simon was minuscule compared to the wide-open gap into the real Simon I was getting now. I muttered something like "cool" but felt anything I could say would fall short of the moment. He stood lost in his faraway time, and then, as if the music mysteriously came echoing through the trees, he was dancing with the beautiful girl from Seattle. His left arm was in front of him leveled at shoulder height and his right around her waist. He two-stepped around the beach, and I think he heard nothing but "The Tennessee Waltz." Derek and Mike stood on the deck of the raft, their arms dropped to their sides for an instant as they watched the would-be ballroom in the sand. After a few more dance moves, Simon twisted and in a single motion bent his knees, picked up a handful of paddles, and stepped toward the raft to deliver that important package. I kept my eyes straight ahead, hoping to mask my utter bewilderment. Then I slightly dropped my chin, turned, pointed my shoulders toward the bank, and walked out of that ballroom forever.

22

The plywood was lashed tightly to the back of the raft, and on top, a stack of sleeping mats cushioned the ride. Derek had fastened packing straps to the raft's metal frame, and they were tightened securely across Keith and over his red life jacket. Then the raft pushed off into the deep, slow-running pool in front of the campsite. Derek sat in the center perch fully in control of the craft with both hands on the oars while the younger guide that usually ran the raft was in the back with Keith. After about five hundred yards, I heard the roar of the rapid.

"Run it down the right side through those small waves, and as soon as you hit the first big one, point your bow left and paddle hard across the river," Mike said. "The current runs into a big rock and you want to miss it—the rock, that is. Derek is not sure how it will actually run in this high water, but past that rock there shouldn't be any obstacles, just a lot of fast water. Eddy out on the right downstream and let's regroup."

Simon hit the first waves and cut through them with speed and momentum. His paddle dug into the gurgling flow on the left and pushed forward slightly in a back paddle motion. His boat lurched left, and he hit the next wave head-on with the big rock safely off his right gunnel. The current pulled Sonia into the first wave a little cockeyed, which threw the nose of the boat to the right. She stuck her paddle deep into the water and executed a firm back stroke. The nose jutted left but the wave washed her into the big rock. She converted the left back paddle to a hard forward stroke and leaned her body into the rock. The boat leveled out like a miracle from heaven. The water smashing into the rock flowed under her boat and lifted it off the rock's rounded surface and into the four-foot hole below it. The bow of her boat crashed into the depression, and the wave seemed to tower over Sonia and the rubber boat. She leaned forward and dug her paddle into the middle of the looming wave and pulled forward. The wave collapsed over the bow of her boat, but she easily punched through to the quiet water below.

I hit the first waves with determination and confidence. As I descended toward the big roller, a series of small waves tossed my bow sideways, throwing me out of control into the wave and toward the rock, forcing a back paddle on the left to regain a cross-river direction, but the rush of water was too strong, lifting my boat up and onto the polished granite surface. Then, like yesterday, I made the fatal mistake. I leaned away from the rock and the boat rolled, exposing the inside cavity to the rushing current. I came out of the boat like a teddy bear in a wind storm. The big wave below the rock curled forward with a force under the surface that pitched me to the bottom of the river. Holding a deep breath, I relaxed and felt the flow get slower as I descended toward the bottom. The slower current carried me beyond the danger, and I popped to the surface about ten feet downstream.

Grabbing the side of Mike's boat, I pulled myself across his bow and just laid there catching my breath as he moved us to the eddy to wait for the raft to shoot the rapid.

My confidence shaken and my lungs still gasping for air, I heard Mike say in a low, quiet voice, "Good place for trout, got everything they need right here, just need four things and it's Mecca-city for fish."

Mike was small talking to calm me down and probably himself too. Nobody could be interested in fishing in a swollen, flooded river with injuries and uncertainties and Keith about to die—not even Mike, I thought.

"Four things. Miss even one and they go someplace else," he continued. "Plenty of oxygen, and the fast water provides that, the colder the better. Warm water doesn't hold the air. They've got to have cover, like brush or trees or a rock ledge or even deep water works all right. The fast water brings food supplies, bugs and all the rest, and they have to have relief from the current. The current looks fast on the surface, but in deeper spots it slows underneath and small rocks on the bottom slow the flow. Yeah, pretty good spot right here."

Just then Simon brought my kayak over, and I climbed into the river-drenched seat as we watched the raft enter the fast water. Derek steered the left pontoon into the first waves, and the boat rocked gently side to side. A simultaneous back stroke on the left and a hard forward paddle on the right swung the front of the boat around, pointing across the river. A couple of power strokes thrust the raft into the big wave, and it skipped over the water to the top of the curl and stopped all forward motion, just surfing the wave. On the boat, Derek looked confident and calm, but a glance over at Sonia was a different story. She had stopped all motion, and her eyes were fixed on the raft. Eventually it slid off the center and into the big rock. Derek reacted quickly with a hard back stroke, causing the pontoon to bounce off the rock surface and rotate into the lower curl with a half turn. The stern collapsed into the hole sideways, but straightened when it hit the wave thanks to another quick paddle stroke. The raft floated in next to us, and Derek checked on Keith, whose wide eyes betrayed his helpless, hysterical fear.

Ten minutes later we pulled into the Horsecreek campground, which spread out a thousand yards into a flat, wide canyon looking like a small delta of sand and small brush. The kayaks lined up on the beach while Keith was moved onto the sand. Sonia rushed over but found him barely able to focus, his eyes opening only occasionally.

"They better get here quick or we're gong to lose him," she whispered.

"I called in to the airport right after we cleared Gunbarrel. They're in the air now. You guys pull the raft under that tree and cinch it up. When the chopper touches down, the rotors will airlift these boats," Derek said like the captain of the USS *Whatever*.

"So these kayaks are goners?" I asked, wishing I had kept my mouth shut.

"The kayaks with you guys in them will be floating down the river when that bird lands," Derek continued. "Get everything you need and get ready to push off. Pick a spot and wait for me downstream. The vans will meet us at a takeout spot in about a mile. Not as fancy as the one I promised yesterday, but it'll do."

We found a quiet stretch to wait downstream and could hear the rotary blades of the helicopter cutting through the moist morning air. The branches bent and flexed in a wild flurry of hysterical motion as the chopper disappeared from our line of sight under the tree line, touching down on the littered sand beach. In no more than five minutes, the air began churning again, and the helicopter rose above us in near vertical flight. I kept my eyes glued to the horizon as the chopper flew up and out, transforming into a small dot and disappearing over the canyon rim.

23

The sun was low when we finished loading the vans and started up the narrow, winding, one-lane road to the highway above. In two hours we pulled into a motel in McCall. Dressed up twenty-somethings strolled into the jazz club next door, and a new strip mall marquis advertised the usual discount stores across the street. Civilization never looked so un-civilized to me, I thought, while I helped unload the duffels. Sonia walked out of the lobby and handed each one of us a magnetic card key.

"Gentlemen, your rooms are ready," she said with a sheepish grin.

Simon reached out through obvious exhaustion, hugged her, and gave her a fatherly kiss on the cheek. No words needed to be spoken, as each worn-out river rat grabbed his bag and disappeared through the lobby. I threw my duffel on my shoulder and headed for room 382. Dropping my bag into an empty elevator, the third-floor button lit up as I gave it a sharp stab. I don't even have her phone number, I thought. What difference does it make? A fling is a fling. Los Angeles is full of more exciting men than me. I'm almost old enough to be her father. But God, does she make me feel young and even a little reckless, I mused. Reckless, what a thought—a serious get-a-way vacation turned into hapless mayhem. Anyway, the kids would kill me if I hooked up with Sonia. Too young.

The card key glided into the narrow slit, a green dot flashed on the handle, and the door opened quietly. I tossed my bag next to the closet and looked up to see a bottle of champagne in a small, green plastic ice bucket on the credenza. Pretty nice for an Econo hotel, I thought to myself.

"Thought you'd never show up," I heard her say.

Propped up with two pillows on the bed in TV-watching position, Sonia sat, still in camp shorts and a T-shirt. I walked over and sat on the bed next to her.

"Derek just called. It's about Keith," she said guardedly and then paused.

I felt the blood rush from my head to my feet along with a sharp, low jab in my temples.

"He made it to the hospital in McCall, and they're moving him to Boise tomorrow. He's going to make it."

"Thank God," I said as I dropped my chin and closed my eyes.

Neither one of us said a word. The silence said everything about the relief we felt. I kicked my shoes off, reached for the champagne, and brought two glasses over and sat next to the bed stand.

Looking directly into her eyes, I took her hand in mine and said, "Lillykile beer?"

"Yeah, well, my dad was the creative type," she said with a slight wink.

"Did all his stories have morbid moral lessons?" I asked.

"He was a rugged individualist. What can I say? He was my dad," she said in nearly a whisper.

Then I leaned down and kissed her hand politely like you would the hand of a queen. I kissed her wrist and gently moved to the soft skin inside her forearm. Opening my mouth, I let my teeth softly bear down upon her arm as if biting her and then grunted playfully. My left hand darted to her rib cage, and my fingers dug tenderly into the soft, ticklish skin. She started to roll her body and thrash at the same time. Like a flash, her hands found the soft, underarm flesh covering my ribs.

"You're dead meat, mister!" she shouted.

I rolled over, trying to pull away from her devilish tickle, but she rolled on top of me and then suddenly stopped. I lifted my head off the pillow and kissed her. The shopping center lights peeked through a crack in the drawn curtains, and there was a faint hint of jazz from below. Just enough civilization, I thought.